The Fortress | Jonathan Hillinger

The Fortress is dedicated to the Hillinger family: Michal, Miriam, Simona, and David, who encouraged me to spread my wings and fly.

To the guiding light in my life, my wife, Patricia, and my two little angels, Sarah and Gabriel, who give me so much inspiration.

In loving memory of Nelu Nazarin and his everlasting smile; to all Holocaust victims, among them my grandfather's mother and sister, Maria and Zsuzsika, who both perished in Auschwitz.

To my grandfather Gabriel and his father Emil who managed to survive the inferno.

And to every child and adult, whoever and wherever they may be - though the way be arduous and exhausting - never stop believing.

The Fortress
Jonathan Hillinger

Translation from the Hebrew: Jerry Hyman
Contact: thefortressyh@gmail.com

ISBN 9781792673276

THE
FORTRESS

Jonathan Hillinger

PROLOGUE

The boy was from a village near Bucharest. His father had started drinking when he lost his job at the factory after it was closed by the government. He would come home drunk every night and take out his frustration on his son, lashing out at him until he tired of it, and would fall into a drunken stupor on the couch.

One morning the boy decided to run away. He packed some clothes into a sack to take with him while his father was lying dead drunk on the sofa in the living room, in a deep sleep from the Ţuică[1]. The boy took his grandfather's cap and stood motionless in the doorway. His mother was in the living room, on the rocking chair, staring blankly at the wall. His sister was still asleep. He entered her room quietly and left a farewell note beside her pillow.

He put on the cap, looked out toward the road, and then looked back sadly - he was leaving his mother and sister behind, but he couldn't go on living like this, so he promised himself that he wouldn't take his cap off until the day he'd come back for them.

He left without looking back, walked from his house toward the railroad tracks that ran along the edge of the village, crawled through an opening in the fence and waited unseen in

---

1   Popular Romanian alcoholic drink

the bushes for a freight train to come by. He spied one on the horizon, coming down the tracks, but his legs wouldn't budge! Fear held them rooted to the ground. The train was getting closer and was about to pass him by, he knew that there was no other choice. Finally, his will overcame his fear and he ran toward one of the cars that was partially open, and darted in. He lay down on the dusty floor inside the dark, gloomy car on his way to Bucharest.

He could not have imagined what would await him when the train got to the station in the center of Bucharest. He had spent his whole life in the village and was now suddenly alone in the big city. The crowd of hustlers he encountered on his way out of the train station scared him, and he hurried out of the station. He didn't know where to turn, but he felt he had to get away, out to the main street and onto one of the side streets. He wandered through the streets until it got dark, trying to get used to the suspicious types he saw, the commotion, the flash of lights. Finally, he slipped down an alley and began gathering cartons to make a simple shelter to sleep in. He never forgot that first night in Bucharest - the temperature dropped below zero. He took off his coat and put on all the clothes he had brought with him, and then wrapped himself up in his coat again. He pulled the cartons around him as close as he could, but the cold penetrated his bones as if to tell him, "Tonight you won't sleep, my friend, not while I'm here." Wide awake and shivering, he waited for dawn. The next morning, he left the improvised shelter and walked toward the end of the alley, lured by the sweet aroma of fresh pastries. He peered in the direction of a small *cofetarie*[2] nearby. For two hours, he stood

---

2   *Cofetarie* – a pastry shop unique to Romania, serving fresh pastries and beverages

there, trying to summon the courage to enter. He had only a few coins in his pocket, and he was afraid he would be told to go away. He just wanted something to eat and wanted to save the dry piece of bread in his bag as long as possible.

"Would you like some pastry?"

The boy looked up. A little man with a large mustache stood beside him.

"Wha...wha...what?"

The man glanced at the stack of cartons a few feet away.

"Did you sleep there last night, boy?"

He did not know what to answer. He didn't want to get in trouble - he had just arrived in Bucharest and was already in a jam. "Run, run," the words pounded in his head, but the man's voice was soft and kind, so he decided to try his luck and start a conversation.

"Yes, but the cartons were here already. I didn't take them from anyone, and I wasn't thinking of taking them with me."

The man smiled and held out his hand.

"I'm Alex."

The boy hesitated for a moment.

"Don't be afraid, you're in good hands. Haven't you heard you can always trust people with mustaches?" He said, smiling.

The boy reached out and shook the man's hand.

"Come in, we'll eat something in the cofetarie, what do you say?"

"I don't want to be any trouble, maybe I should wait outside."

"Don't worry, I'll take you, no one will say anything, I have an 'in' with the owner," he said, winking at him.

They went into the shop, and the young man at the counter greeted the man with the mustache.

"Good morning, Mr. Eminescu!"

"Good morning, how are we doing today?"

"Everything's fine, we've just taken out the *prajituri* and *fursecuri*.[3]"

"Oh, there's nothing like some fresh goodies and a cup of tea to start the day, right?" He said to the boy and winked again. The boy nodded. The man went behind the counter and returned with a plate of four round biscuits and a cup of tea.

Two of the cookies were topped with red jam, and the others were almost completely filled with chocolate.

"This is for you."

"How come you're allowed to go behind the counter and get yourself cookies just like that?"

"Don't tell anybody, but the owner is allowed." This time, when the man smiled at him, he smiled back, and reached for the plate. They were the most delicious cookies he had ever eaten. "Want some more?"

"No, thanks... really thank you... I wanted to ask... maybe... you're looking for some workers"...?

"You're a little too young to be looking for a job, aren't you?" The boy thought he had crossed the line and didn't want to get himself into trouble.

"Oh, well... sorry... I'll go now."

The boy got up from the chair at the counter, but the man put his hand on his shoulder to sit him back down.

"Listen, I can always use someone to help to clean up around here. How would you like to help me when the cofetarie is open? I'll pay you a few *lei*.[4]"

The two shook hands closing the 'deal'.

---

3   *Prajituri* and *fursecuri* - Romanian cakes and cookies

4   A Romanian coin

"That's fine," said the boy.

"And I'll give you a few more lei if you stay in the back of the store at night. There's a problem with the lock, and I don't want anyone to break in. So if anything happens, you'll be there to make some noise and run quick to call me. Think you can handle that?"

"I think so!"

"Come on, I'll show you the storeroom."

The two of them went behind the counter, and the man led him into a small, warm room.

"It's not much, but I'll get you a mattress in here so you'll have something to lay your head on while you keep watch, is that all right?"

"Yes. All right with me."

That very day, Alex and the boy started on a new period in their lives.

Every morning Alex came and woke the boy, who slept in the storeroom. The boy would go to the counter, and eagerly eat a piece of bread and some pastries, then straighten up the place for a new work day to begin.

The boy soon learned when the customers would arrive, and when he needed to help cleaning up and setting up the tables, and did it energetically – to earn his keep. Sometimes, when business was slow in the cofetarie, the boy asked Alex if he could go for a walk in the streets.

"Sure. Take a walk around, get to know the city, just be careful and pay attention to where you're going," he said with a smile and patted the boy's cap.

One day the boy came to a marketplace. It was like the market in his village, but bigger and busier. Amid the crowd of vendors and customers, he noticed a boy, a street kid about his age, wearing ragged clothes. The boy was even thinner than he was. His legs were so skinny it looked like they could barely hold him up. Suddenly, the boy in the tattered clothes went up to an apple stand, took an apple, and put it in quickly in his pocket without paying. The apple vendor saw him and started to chase after him, as the boy ran away in panic he bumped into a passerby and fell down. The stall owner reached the boy and was about to swat him with a stick he had in his hand. The raggedy boy covered his face in terror. When the vendor saw how miserable and fragile looking the child was, how helpless and frightened, he slowly lowered the stick.

"Stay away from my stand, kid!" the man said, moving away.

The boy went over to the kid in the shabby clothes who was still lying on the ground, and tried to help him up.

"I don't need your help!" said the boy with shabby clothes. The boy looked at him and held out an apple in his hand.

"So you won't have to get into trouble with the other stands today."

The raggedy boy looked at him for a moment, grabbed the apple from his hand, and quickly ran off.

***

One day a policeman with a serious expression on his face came into the cofetarie and started talking to Alex. The boy, meantime, was clearing off one of the tables near the entrance and noticed how the policeman looked at him. At one point in the conversation, the policeman pointed towards him. He could not hear the conversation, but fear began to creep into his bones. He put down the mop in his hand and quickly slipped out. He ran to the one place he knew the police would have trouble following him: the marketplace. As he was wandering between the stands, he suddenly saw the raggedy boy again.

"I owe you an apple," said the boy as he approached him, and before he could answer, the boy went on: "If you're so good at grabbing apples, come with me."

The two of them walked for several blocks, and the boy thought he soon wouldn't be able to find his way back to the market or to the cofetarie. Eventually, they stopped in front of a big, beautiful white building.

Before he even knew where he was, the raggedy boy started to drag him with him.

He was struck by the splendor of the building. He was then led through a secret pathway to what seemed to him to be like another world. Soon all the bright beauty was replaced by darkness and dust, as they passed through tunnels and shallow creeks of water. The path did not seem to be leading anywhere but he put his trust in the raggedy boy. He had no other choice. It became clear to him he wouldn't be able to go back to the cofetarie if the police is looking for him.

The dark trail led into a dimly lit tunnel.

"Don't worry, just a little farther and we're there," the raggedy boy said. When they reached the end of the tunnel, the boy stood motionless and looked around him. He could not believe his eyes.

"Welcome to The Fortress," said the raggedy boy. "By the way, my name is Dumitru, but everybody calls me Mitu."

"N… N… Nice to meet you," said the boy, still wonderstruck at what he was seeing, and finding it hard to get the words out of his mouth… "I… I'm Nelu."

CHAPTER 2

I Am Daniel

As a child, the world is your playground. As a teenager, you think you can conquer it. I was just at that time of life in which the greatest lessons are learned - between childhood and maturity. The whole world was at my feet. I experienced the happiness and optimism that only the innocence of childhood can offer. I had a wonderful family and a promising future. Nothing could have prepared me for what was to come. I grew up in Bucharest in the days after the First World War. These were prosperous times for Romania, both culturally and economically, particularly in Bucharest, and especially for minorities. There was a sense of a change in the air: According to the 1919 Paris Peace Conference: "Romania undertakes to recognize the rights of Romanian citizens, without formalities, including Jews living in Romania who cannot claim another nationality." One year later, the King of Romania issued an order to grant civil rights to all minorities.

My father was a banker, which allowed us to live in a spacious apartment on Calea Grivitei, near the spectacular Calea Victoriei. The city was built according to Parisian architecture, and therefore was called the "Paris of the east." I lived in the apartment on Calea Grivitei with my father, Constantin, my mother, Clara, and my little sister Liliana (Lili). I do not know if my parents had planned it, but one of the most impressive buildings in Bucharest and in all of Romania was a 15-minute walk away, at number 1 Benjamin Franklin Strada.

I was seven years old when I first saw it, and I'll never forget it.

My father woke me up early and whispered in my ear: "Today I have a surprise for you. I need you to get up and get dressed quickly so we can leave on time." Despite this instruction, I arose slowly from my comfortable bed and went to the kitchen for breakfast. It was Sunday, and Sunday breakfast meant *salată de boeuf,*[5] eggs, bread and butter, and for dessert, my favorite, *placinta cu dovleac*[6]. My father urged me to hurry and in my impetuosity, I almost scalded my tongue when I drank my tea. If I had known what awaited me that day, I would not have wasted a minute!

We left my mother at home with my sister - who was barely two years old - and went out the door. My father led me down Calea Grivitei towards the intersection with Calea Victoriei. The way seemed endless and my patience was worn out within ten minutes. I started asking my father over and over if we were there yet, and I must have repeated the question nonstop, because my father, who was not an easy person to ruffle, got fed up with answering me.

"Soon!" he said, and looked at me sternly. I realized I'd

---

5   *Salată de boeuf* (English: *Beef salad*) is a traditional Romanian dish, generally served during all festive and special occasions. It is a combination of finely chopped beef (or sometimes chicken, or turkey breast) and root vegetables, folded in mayonnaise and finished with *murături*, pickled vegetable garnishes

6   *Placinta cu dovleac* = pumpkin pie

better keep quiet until we got there..

We passed Strada Episcopiei, then Strada Piata, and turned left towards Strada Benjamin Franklin. I thought we would never get there. At that point my father finally stopped.

"You see? I told you we'd be there soon." I looked all around me, trying to see what the surprise was. I spotted a sculpted whitewashed sidewalk with beautiful trees planted at its curb, and then I noticed that my father had halted in front of a fence with white stone columns, a gate in the middle and white statues on either side.

Beyond the gate was an enormous lawn the size and shape of a soccer field. We went inside the gate. The lawn was adorned with flowerbeds in a myriad of colors, and lined on both sides with stone paths and rows of trees. The trees' bright green color stood out strongly against the white of the building. It was not until we walked on farther that I noticed the enormous structure that rose up behind the lawn. It looked to me as if all of Bucharest could be hidden behind it. Stunned by the sight, I stopped about forty yards away, trying to take in the splendor of this building in its entirety. It was by far the most beautiful thing I had ever seen in my seven years of life. A few stairs led up to the building entrance, at the top of which was a line of marble columns set close together. Behind the columns were enormous glistening wooden doors, topped by round windows decorated with colorful paintings of regal figures. The columns stretched upward until they were joined by circular, chiseled joints, rising to a triangular roof, on which was a large stone dome engraved with large letters. Slowly, I read the inscription: 'A-t-e-n-e-u-l R-o-m-a-n'. I turned my gaze to the side of the building to see where it ended and I couldn't – it appeared to extend farther and farther with no end in sight. When I turned to my right, I saw my father looking at me with a big smile on his face.

"Do you like what you see Daniel?"

I couldn't get the words out at first, I was so dazzled by the beauty of the place, and I just nodded my head.

After a few seconds I pulled myself together and asked, "What is this place, father?"

"This place is called the *Ateneul Român*, Daniel. It is Bucharest's concert hall where the Philharmonic orchestra plays, and where our finest culture is presented. Your mother and I used to come here long before you and Lili were born. We're going to resume this custom with you, so I brought you along with me today. What do you think? Shall we enter?"

I gladly agreed, and we went in through the main doors. From that moment, my fate was tied to the fate of the Athenaeum. It was only when we went up the stairs that I noticed the crowd entering through the big doors. As we passed by them, a luxurious reception hall unfolded before my eyes. The floor was gleaming white, with countless colorful shapes on it. Along the sides of the hall were square inlaid brown panels, followed by green and yellow circles all around the center of the hall. The magnificent ceiling was adorned with huge paintings and enormous chandeliers that illuminated the entire reception hall. White with brown-hued marble pillars reached from the floor to the ceiling. Row by row, the pillars grew more rose-colored, until they became pink at the very end of the hall. They ended in splendid arches with gilded decorations on varied backgrounds, some in red and others in shades of white.

On each side of the hall there were stairways leading to the upper and lower areas. The stairs were spirals decorated in green and brown lines, topped with beautifully carved stones. The hall began to fill with people, and my father took me toward one of three entrances to the concert hall. The concert hall was even bigger and more elegant than the entrance hall. My father led me toward the red rows of seats in the center of the hall and we sat down. I looked around me. People began to settle into their places. I looked up at the walls. The hall was encircled by walls covered with majestic murals, as if they were trying to tell a story. I followed the paintings with my eyes: knights fighting on a battlefield; then knights mounted on horses with the common people cheering them on. They led me to imagine myself as one the knights returning home to the accolades and cheers of the people. Above the paintings, the walls were decorated in gold and marble and rose up higher and higher toward the enormous dome of the concert hall. A large, ornate chandelier hung from the top, illuminating the entire space.

I looked towards the stage. The large red curtain was closed and at both ends were statues of angels carrying a harp. The lights dimmed and the concert hall darkened. Total silence.

My father leaned toward me and whispered, "Ready?"

I looked at my father and nodded, and as if he had coordinated it with the stage crew, at that very moment, the red curtain parted in the middle and the center of the stage was illuminated in the spotlight. At center stage stood a young man with a violin on his left shoulder. In his right hand was a bow that he slowly raised toward the instrument. The moment the bow touched the strings of the violin, a sound broke the silence that seemed to pierce through my body. I could not believe that such a small object could produce such wonderful sounds. I stared, fascinated at his every movement. The chords and melody that came out of the instrument were so pure, it was as if the music embraced me and swept away everything else.

I imagined myself floating up out of my seat and becoming the artist himself. I was the one on the stage, and everyone sat in perfect silence, watching and listening to me play. It was magnificent and I was hypnotized. Never before had music made me feel that way, so touching and so pure. Only when the artist had stopped playing and bowed as the crowd rose to its feet to applaud did I realize he had finished. I looked at my father and we both stood up and joined in the applause. An announcer came on and said something but I couldn't hear a thing because of the applause that lasted several minutes. The young violinist finished bowing to the audience and left the stage. Slowly, people began to exit the hall. Before my father could say anything, I grabbed at his sleeve and he looked at me.

"Father, who was the man who played the violin?"

"Did you like the music?"

"Yes! A lot! Maybe one day I'll be a violin player and everyone will come to see me appear here!"

My father smiled at me. "Maybe you will.

"The man you heard playing is a great violinist named George Enescu."

And so it came about that when I was seven years of age, the great George Enescu made me float high above my seat in the concert hall to the heavenly sounds of a violin solo, even though I did not know much about Bach or classical music of any kind. Later, a street leading to the Athenaeum would be named after him. No wonder that from that day I waited impatiently for the weekends we went to the Athenaeum. On Friday evenings my father used to take us to the synagogue in the Calea Văcăreşti (in Văcăreşti neighborhood) and Bradului Strada. It was a long walk, but my father insisted. "We come on foot to greet the Sabbath at the synagogue," he would answer when I asked why we didn't drive there. Only years later did I understand.

Sundays were devoted to a walk with the family. My mother would make a meal and pack it in a large basket, with a cloth spread over it to keep it fresh. We took the food with us on a walk along the boulevard on the banks of the Dâmboviţa River. We would sit on one of the benches under the trees and eat everything my mother had prepared. As the years went by and I grew up, the smaller the Athenaeum seemed to me. Yet every time I walked through the big wooden doors at the entrance, I would have the same sense of magic that arose in me the first time I set foot in the reception hall. Sometimes I visited the place by myself, to check on upcoming performances to tell the family about, but mostly I came just for the feeling, the magical feeling that the Athenaeum always aroused in me.

We have witnessed countless performances: The pianist Dinu Lipatti, Constantin Tanase the entertainer, the singer Maria Tanase, the violinist Grigoras Dinicu and many other great artists. I never imagined back then, that grim, fateful days would come along and change everything...

***

When I turned fifteen, we all gathered in my house: my father and mother, Lili my sister, Ion, Andrei, and Lucian, my good friends from school, Catia and me. I met Catia at the age of fourteen by chance. One time when we were in the synagogue, I slipped outside without my father noticing. I wandered out on Bradului Strada until I came to a cofetarie and went in. As soon as I entered, a guitar caught my eye. It was leaning against the right side of the counter. Guitars have always fascinated me, although I never had a chance to play one. I went up to the counter and glanced at the waiter.

"Can I take a look at the guitar?"

"You'll have to ask the owner."

"Isn't it yours?"

"No, but the owner is standing right behind you." I looked back, and there was a smiling girl with long, dark brown hair. She had a pair of big brown eyes that seemed to encompass a whole world within. Her smile was full of light. Everything around her seemed to fade in her shining presence. I think it's safe to say I was dazzled by her right from the first moment I saw her. I wanted to say something clever or pleasant, but instead of words from the myriad letters running through my head, only a few stuttering syllables and consonants emerged:

"Is... guitar? ...uh, what... can I... p-play a... little... uh..." It was clear from the look she gave me that she was trying to figure out if I had some kind of speech impediment, but luckily, it did not stop her, and she started a conversation with me:

"It's a pretty guitar, isn't it? It's new and I'm just starting to learn how to play it - can you play the guitar?"

"Yes," I lied, because if she had asked me if cows could fly I would have said yes.

"Wow, so maybe you can teach me. Do you live around here?"

"Yes, I mean, no," I answered, showing once again my command of the language.

"Is it yes or no?"

"We always come on Fridays to the synagogue, but I live in

Griviței Road in the center, it's a little far from here."

"Griviței? It is far, so maybe you can come someday to visit. Do you have a bicycle?"

"Yes!" At least this time I didn't lie.

"Come on, I'll show you where I live." She took my hand, and we immediately left the cofetarie. Ever since then, even without knowing where we were going, I followed her.

She was like one of my family and I became like one of hers. In the end, she was the one who taught me to play the guitar, and I learned very quickly. Sometimes I would melt looking into her eyes without and then suddenly come out of it without her ever noticing. Our houses were twenty minutes away from each other by bicycle. We would race each other, and to be honest, even when I really tried, she always beat me. We became best friends.

Her mother, Adela, liked me very much. She would often ask me about school, and how things were going at my house. She wasn't just being polite, she was genuinely interested. She was one of those unique people who could listen in a remarkable way, and it made me feel comfortable to be around her. When we would leave Catia's house, her mother always bid me goodbye the same way: she would turn to me and say, "Daniel, Take care of my Catia, all right?" and I would nod my head yes. Finally, it became such a habit that she made do only with a special look, and I would just nod.

Sometimes Catia and I would go off together for the day. We always found lots to do, but her parents instructed us to come home before dark. One day, while we were lying sprawled on the grass in the park, Catia asked me:

"Have you ever kissed anyone?" For a boy of fifteen, especially for one who had only ever kissed his mother, there was no way to answer such a question without feeling ashamed, and sure enough, I started blushing. I tried to think how I could evade answering truthfully.

"Uh... I... if... uh..."

"It must be interesting," she said without even listening to what I said... or tried to say. Before I could even think of anything, she leaned over to me and kissed me.

"What do you think of that?" She said.

I just nodded. If I had been honest, I could have told her I heard birds singing in my heart.

"Maybe... we should ...try it again," I said, kissing her. Catia, with her beautiful bright smile, got up and reached out a hand to me to help me up.

"We have to go back, or my parents will worry." Time? I wasn't thinking about the time. Time stood still those last few moments. People say you cannot stop time, but when your hearts skips a beat, it seems to.

On the day of my fifteenth birthday, my father invited my friends to all go together to the Athenaeum to celebrate.

After a routine party at home—sitting around the table, telling jokes and eating the birthday cake my mother always insisted on making (because as a child she had never had a birthday cake), we got organized and went off to the Athenaeum.

When we arrived, we found there was a long line at the ticket counter in the reception hall. We stood in the line and slowly advanced, continuing our mood of celebration. Ion, Andrei, Lucian, and I were laughing and joking all the time. Catia smiled nonstop, and I did not need anything more than that to keep up my good mood. Catia asked to excuse her as she went to the restroom, which was located down the hall and then down the staircase on the left side of the reception hall.

The rest of us continued talking and laughing.

During those few minutes, I had noticed two raggedy young boys roaming around the reception hall through the crowd. They caught my eye mainly because the way they were dressed was out of place in such splendid surroundings. However, I lost sight of them when they were swallowed up by the crowd, and the conversation with my father made me forget all about them. Then, suddenly, about ten minutes after Catia had gone, I heard shouting from afar. I interrupted my conversation with my father in an attempt to isolate the source of the noise from the clamor of the crowd in the reception hall. I heard a second scream that I had no doubt had come from the corridor. I ran over to the area quickly. When I heard the third scream, I knew it was Catia. I hurried down the stairs. The shouts became clearer and sharper until I reached the bottom of the stairwell where I stopped in amazement. The two punks I had noticed before in the reception hall were trying to wrestle Catia's purse away from her. They had no idea what a struggle they would get from her! One boy had glasses and short, wiry hair, and the other was wearing a brown cap.

I threw myself at them and blocked the passageway to the stairs. One of the punks saw me and managed to snatch the bag out of her hands. He started running with it towards the bathroom at the end of the corridor on the right and the other boy followed him. I started running. First toward Catia to see if she was okay, and then towards the punks that ran to the restroom, together with Catia. Before going in, I told Catia to call the ushers and she did. I knew that if I spoke to her with logic she would listen and not insist on going in with me. I knew they had to be hiding in one of the toilet stalls and I stooped to see if there were legs under the doors, but all the stalls seemed empty. I guessed that the two punks were standing on the toilet seats so I wouldn't see them.

I yelled, "You better come out! You can't get away!" I opened the first stall slowly, thinking maybe they might jump at me, but it was empty. I opened the next one slowly, and the creaking door seemed to be a warning sign… but again, there was no one in the stall. I reached the last one, took a deep breath and pulled the door open furiously, but to my surprise… empty. I checked all the toilets and stalls again. There was no other place to hide in the bathroom. The two punks were gone as if the earth had swallowed them up.

The ushers got to the bathroom entrance along with Catia, Ion, Andrei and Lucian, who had heard the shouts and saw us running down the corridor. We started to explain what had happened. I was angry that the ushers hadn't noticed the two punks right away. The embarrassed ushers said that this was not the first time it happened that there was a theft before the start of a performance - it had happened a few times that they were told there were some troublemakers milling around the crowd. The ushers did not understand how time after time the thieves managed to slip away from them. Catia was upset. She kept an embroidered handkerchief in her purse that had belonged to her grandmother.

I did not know how to console her, but she quickly recovered, put a smile on her face and said: "Well, is it your birthday or not? We came to enjoy ourselves, so let's enjoy! Forget about it!" and she took my hand and signaled us all to go back to the line in the hall. I had no intention of forgetting what had happened, but I followed her and together we walked back up to the reception hall, where my father was waiting with the tickets.

"Is everything all right, Catia?" my father asked.

"Everything's fine."

We went in. She did not even tell him what happened. Catia insisted that she was all right, but I could see on her face that she was not. I waited until the intermission and jumped out of my seat with the excuse that I needed to go to the bathroom. I got to the toilet area. I could still hear the low rumble from the audience in the big hall. I checked every inch of the bathroom again. How in one moment those two punks were right before my eyes and then suddenly disappear? I couldn't figure it out... I glanced toward the ventilation duct. It was covered with iron mesh screwed on over the opening. It looked like it would be near impossible to remove those screws, I felt discouraged.

I leaned despairingly against the wall near the entrance to the bathroom just before returning to the hall. Suddenly, my right hand felt a bulge in the wall that continued along the length of the wall. It was a little less than a meter long, and at the end, it went vertically downward about half a meter. It was a wooden board painted the same color of the wall. I tried to grip it by the edges and pull it off with my fingers, but I couldn't. I kept trying. After a few minutes, I felt the board move slightly in my direction. I tried harder - another little bit, and another inch, and slowly the board came loose and I could grab the end of it and yank it off the wall. I finally tore the board off the wall and threw it on the floor. In front of me was a dark tunnel about sixty centimeters in diameter. It looked deep, but it was hard to know because of the darkness within. I finally understood how they disappeared; now I needed to know where.

I crawled into the tunnel, dragging myself inside. The light from the bathroom became fainter as I moved farther into the tunnel. After about ten meters, I had to feel my way forward. Suddenly I felt the rough, crumbling stone that my hands had been scraping below me was gone. My hands caught air, and so did the underside of my body - the space on which I was crawling ended. I had to stretch out my arm below me to feel the ground again. The tunnel I crawled from ended in a larger, darker space. It was almost pitch black as I crawled my way out of the tunnel. Initially on all fours, and then I realized I could stand. I uncurled my legs and slowly straightened up. I thought about going back, but I had a goal, even while I was dragging myself through the darkness. If there was the slightest chance I could find them, I had to try.

I started to move a little forward, step by step, one foot after the other. The faint light that came from the tunnel from which I had emerged was almost obliterated in the darkness, but I could still see a little bit on the side. Suddenly, the light disappeared in a flash and the darkness became absolute. I took two more steps. In absolute silence around me, I began to hear the sound of the soles of shoes rubbing against the ground. I realized I was not alone…

CHAPTER 3

I Am Nelu

It was evening on a performance day. Matei wanted Mitu and me to take a spin around the "ring" —that's what he called it—and when Matei said something while holding his staff in his hand, there was no room for argument. I did not like the idea. The ring was the concert hall, and lately Matei had decided it was possible to take the risk and send someone around in the crowd to try to come back with some loot. Nicu and Matei were the first to take a spin, and, so as not to return empty-handed, or perhaps simply because they wanted to, they returned with two purses, and suddenly it became the norm: to come back with at least one wallet each time. The idea was simple. You take a spin around the ring, choose a wealthy looking person, and one of us would "bump" into him or her while the other one comes from behind and yanks out a wallet or a purse. I yanked out some food to survive, but stealing wallets did not seem to me as a survival necessity, but more Matei's whim. Moreover, if you wanted to remain part of the gang, you had to do what Matei said. When Mitu and I were sent, we usually did not return with much loot. It had already happened that people spotted us and we had to run away. A few times, they almost caught us, and it was too risky.

One day we wandered around undisturbed searching for easy targets. Mitu had managed to steal a wallet from a man I bumped into in the reception hall, and then he saw a young woman walking toward the bathroom. He nudged my shoulder to get my attention.

"Let's follow her, she's going toward the bathroom, that's the closest there is to The Fortress – the quickest job we'll ever do. You can grab her bag and get away easily."

"Mitu, it's not a good idea. She is young and we'll scare her. The fact you pick people's pockets without their noticing is one thing, but when you want to attack somebody, that's something else."

"Baloney, it's all the same bullshit." Mitu was already pursuing her into the bathroom and I had no choice but to follow him and try to persuade him not to do it. Before I could reach him, he had already slipped away from the crowd and had gone down the stairs. The corridor was empty and the girl was on her way into the bathroom.

"Listen, Mitu, this is not a good idea! Let's go back up, we'll snag two wallets. To ambush a girl like this, it's not right."

"Stop whining and come on! You'll see it's easy."

We went down the stairs, but there was no one in the corridor. She had probably gone into the bathroom.

"Anyway, Mitu, we have to get back already, we could end up being seen here."

"Don't start, Nelu, Matei could get annoyed, and I can't take his nerves and listen to his threats."

"Mitu, I understand that he seems to be in charge of us, and I don't want…"

"Nelu, don't start with this talk, we do our share like everybody else and that's it. You know that's how it works."

"Things can be done differently, Mitu... but never mind, it doesn't matter. Come on, we'll just go back... if he starts getting mad, I promise I'll take the blame. Let's just go back."

We were already on our way back, when the girl came out of the bathroom. Mitu ran quickly towards her, and tried to snatch her bag. I could see he had not expected such a strong reaction from a young girl: she pulled her arm away and grabbed the bag back and started screaming. Mitu pulled on the bag as hard as he could, but he could not get it away from her, and she kept yelling. It was only a matter of time before we would get caught.

"Mitu let it go!" But Mitu was determined to prove to me that this was not a bad idea. I had no choice but to grab Mitu and try to get him to let go of the girl's arm. It had already gone too far. Suddenly, someone ran down the hall and shouted at us. The girl's attention was diverted for a moment, and Mitu took advantage of it to get the bag away from her. He ran towards the bathroom with me right behind him. We removed the cover to the tunnel and entered. We ran from the first tunnel to the second towards The Fortress.

"Nelu, stop, wait a minute." Mitu grabbed my arm. "I'll hide the bag under my shirt. Not a word to Matei!" I was still in shock by what had happened and agreed, just as long as we were going back.

An hour after we returned, sitting alone in the cave, Mitu looked around to make sure there was no one watching us, and opened the bag. There were some candies in the bag, a few coins and some makeup utensils.

"Mitu, that was too close, it's our responsibility to make sure they can't track us down. The girl must have brought the ushers into the bathroom. We have to go back and make sure we didn't leave any traces behind and closed the entrance properly." Mitu agreed. Matei was very clear about that, and rightly so. No one can know about the entrance.

We re-entered the dark tunnel leading to the exit.

"I'm not crawling back to check. You do it, Mitu; you're the one who got us in this mess." Even If the lid were just slightly open, you could notice it since the light was flickering in from the outside into the cave, but I had to send Mitu to look closely and double check that the lid was properly sealed. Mitu had crawled more than half way when suddenly noises were heard from the end of the tunnel. Light had started to creep into the tunnel.

"Mitu! Come back! Now!" Mitu looked up ahead, and then started to turn back in fear. We stood on either side of the cave and saw that the lid had been removed. Someone was there, crawling toward us! We stood quietly in the space between the two tunnels. He couldn't see us, because the darkness between the two tunnels was almost total. Whoever it was, we had to chase him out of there; we had to protect The Fortress. When the person reached the entrance to the passageway, Mitu disappeared. I moved away to the second tunnel. The light entering the tunnel from the outside was suddenly blocked again. I knew it was Mitu. He went back and closed the lid. I didn't know what he planned to do to the intruder, but at that point I put my hand on a flashlight that was permanently set into a crevice in the wall. We left the flashlight there as a guide in and out of the tunnel only for emergencies and this certainly qualified as one.

I heard steps, and then silence. I stopped moving. Again, the sound of footsteps echoed in the cave. This time there were two sets. I heard a shout, I knew it was Mitu. I heard sounds of a struggle. I started moving toward the noises, I knew Mitu needed my help and I couldn't wait any longer. I turned on the flashlight. A shadowy figure was standing over Mitu, who was on the ground.

"Get away from him, and I'll let you go back. If you don't, I'll call the rest of the guys and you'll never get out of here!"

"You want me to release him? Give me back the bag you stole from my friend!"

"We didn't take any bag, leave him alone!" I lied.

He was a young boy like us, but well dressed. He looked agitated, as we probably looked to him. He loosened his grip on Mitu for a second, and Mitu got up quickly and leaped towards me. There was no way to solve the problem we had gotten ourselves into. I quickly switched off the flashlight and Mitu and I ran back to The Fortress in the dark. We saw he wasn't following us, but we had to tell Matei about it. Things weren't easy after this. We were afraid we might be discovered because of what we had done and because of what Matei might do to us. But nothing happened in the next few days. Everything went back to normal and we started to think we could forget it ever happened, but then, the boy came back.

Lizica and Dinu were the first to spot him.

"Matei, Matei! There's an intruder in The Fortress" they shouted. Mitu ran towards the entrance of the tunnel and I followed him. I saw someone coming towards us. I recognized him immediately. It was the same boy who had followed us through the tunnel. Nicu, Doru, and Rita were already walking toward him. Mitu and I went towards the stairs and Lizica and Dinu gathered their courage and joined us. We stood at the center of The Fortress. Matei had told us that if an intruder would get into The Fortress, we should all stand in front of him and be ready. Together it would be hard for anyone to hurt us. He had even shown us where to stand, and that's what we did.

The boy was well dressed, wearing a gray jacket and a buttoned white shirt, gray trousers and polished brown shoes. He had short brown hair and green eyes. He stopped about ten meters from us. Matei stood with the staff in his hand between us and the boy.

"You are in our fortress. Uninvited guests are not welcome here."

"I know this is your secret place. I promise not to tell anyone. I didn't come to hurt anybody. I'm just asking you to give back the white bag you took a week ago. It's very important to me. If you give it back, I won't bother you anymore."

We were silent, looking at him, waiting for Matei to say something. Matei looked over at Nicu and Doru and started laughing.

"I'll find you your white bag, but I don't ever want to see you here again, are we clear?"

The boy nodded in agreement.

"I'll go look for it!" Mitu volunteered and ran toward the room where the loot was stored. After a few minutes of searching in the piles of bags, purses, and clothes we had accumulated, Mitu came out with the white bag. He gave it to Matei and stood back in line. Matei took a step towards the boy, looking at him closely for several seconds, and handed him the bag. We were lucky that Matei was concentrating on the boy's face; otherwise, he might have noticed that the bag had never passed under his scrutiny. The boy took the bag from Matei.

"Thanks." He reached into his pocket and took out some candy.

"This is for you."

Rita didn't think twice, she ran toward him, snatched the candy out of his hand and showed it to Matei.

As the boy turned and started walking back to the tunnel, Matei shouted at him: "You brought four candies and we are eight people. Are we supposed to cut them in half? We don't want your candy! Don't come back here."

The boy hesitated for a moment, but kept walking without looking back, and disappeared into the tunnel.

I couldn't explain it, but I was sad to see him go.

CHAPTER 4

I Am Ionel

I can barely remember my mother. I was four when she died from the illness. It was in 1952, when Gheorghiu-Dej took control over communist Romania. My mother lay in bed for months and could not recover. I remember my father yelling at her that she was being lazy, just staying in bed, and she would sob. Sometimes I thought she has to get better, she can't be sick for so long. However, every time I looked at her suffering face, my hopes were crushed. I knew that she wanted to get up and hug me, to sit with me when I went to bed or even to make me breakfast, but she was too weak. Every time my father shouted at her to get better, I would go to her and ask if she was all right, if she wanted me to bring her something. She would hold my hand, look up at me and say, "My Ionel," with a smile, and I would give her a kiss on the forehead. I thought to myself that if I am so important to her, she will not give up and will fight the sickness, and that meant she would get better.

Bit by bit, my father began to lose interest in her. In the moments she needed us most, he treated her as a nuisance. I would lay my head on her stomach, and she would sing to me while stroking my head, as she used to do every night at my bedside before she fell ill.

I remember hearing the doctor explain to my father that if she had gotten to the hospital sooner there would have been hope, but now the only thing left to do was pray. Whenever I lay down next to her, I would ask her not to forget to be strong for my sake, and she would answer and say that I was the only one for whom she was struggling.

I remember how I wanted to cry when she closed her eyes for the last time and the doctor told us she'd gone, but my father slapped me and told me I had to pull myself together like a man.

I did not want to believe she was dead. I was angry at the world. I was angry because it wasn't fair that all the other kids were happy and I was not, I was angry that I wouldn't ever see her again, I was angry at my father who didn't take care of her with the love she deserved, and I was angry at the doctors who didn't cure her. My nasty father was all that I was left with, and I was not prepared for this reality. Every time I started to sob, he slapped me and said I needed to be a man and not a spoiled child. Only at the funeral did he let me cry, and I broke into tears like never before, because I knew I would not get a second chance. I thought that if I missed her enough, somehow she might come back.

I remember my father at the funeral, standing to the side wearing a suit I had never seen before, with a blank expression on his face. Not grief, not anger. He looked like any one of the other people there, just waiting for it to be over.

It was the first time I realized just how uncaring he was, and I learned to expect nothing more from him. He couldn't send me to school, he couldn't listen to me, and he couldn't hold a job. It was like that before, but now that my mom was gone, it was worse. I was a small child, but I had already lived in many places... My father would move us to different apartments in Bucharest every three months, from one neglected department to another. Before I could get used to a place, we were already moving to another, and they were not easy to get used to. They were in overcrowded old buildings; full of people I was afraid of passing by in the hallways. I would run as fast as I could into the building and down the corridor, to get to our apartment as quickly as possible. The apartments were always tiny, the neighbors were always noisy, and the worst part was that we always shared a bedroom. Sometimes my father would bring a woman to the apartment and move me into the living room. I don't know where I slept more often, in the bedroom or on the foul smelling sofa in the living room. I would drag my mattress with me into the living room so I could fall asleep on it and not on the sofa, trying to ignore all the noises. You could hear everything through the thin walls. It was so awful, the only way I could fall asleep was to bury myself under the blankets and pull the pillow over my ears. He kept telling me I should be thankful for having somewhere to sleep, and I would wonder if God was punishing me because I was not thankful enough.

He would bring home some of the women more than once, and I would think maybe I'll have a new mother, but none of those women looked at me as my mother did...

There were times when he came into the apartment while he was still groping some woman and shrink back for a moment when he saw me, as if he'd forgotten I lived there. As for food, I had to make do with leftovers in the *racitor*[7]. I was

---

7   *Racitor* – before refrigerators, a wooden box packed with ice to keep food cold

often slapped for not leaving him anything to eat, as if there was a lot to begin with.

My father did not care what I did during the day. He never inquired. I spent most of the day in the street trying to figure out what to do, and who to play with... and return to the apartment at night, hoping there was something to eat. Even though there was room in the bed for both of us, he had this little mattress for me that went with us from apartment to apartment that he threw down on the floor near the bed. He would say, "That's what there is, boy." He always called me "boy," as if I weren't his. He slept up in the bed and I was on the mattress on the floor. If I had complained, he would have slapped me before he understood what I was talking about. That's why even when I had a problem, like my constant hunger, I preferred not to tell him. That was the reason that during the day I started to join the street children in the big square. I felt just like them; I saw myself as a street boy like them. I imagined they were like me. That they had a place to live, but just preferred not to be there. One day I went home and found my father fondling a woman who had red hair and wore lots of makeup. As he leaned her up against the table, I remember she glared at me. I did not know exactly why she was staring like that, but I knew she didn't like me being there.

"What is that?" she said. "*What is that*?" Not "Who is that?" like I was a piece of furniture... furniture she did not like.

"It's my kid, don't pay any attention to him." He looked at me angrily. "Don't you have anything to do? Go play in the square, can't you see we're busy?"

"If I had somewhere to go, do you think I would come back here? I don't have anything to do outside," I replied.

When he brought women home, I could let myself answer

him like that. I would never do it when he was alone but I knew he wouldn't hit me in front of them. He pushed himself away from her and the table and looked at me. I knew if she wasn't there, I would have gotten it good. Usually he would come into the bedroom and tell me to find something to do in the living room.

This time, the presence of the woman who did not like me had an effect on him, and he said, "Listen to me, I said go and find something to do, so do it!"

"What am I going to do outside now? I'm tired and I want to go to sleep soon anyway." The woman glared at me again, half in disgust. He went back to what he was doing with her…

"Don't worry, he won't disturb us."

"But he's staying in the apartment?"

He looked at me again.

"Something you didn't understand!? I told you to go out and find something to do!" He went over to my mattress lying in the corner, picked it up, came towards me and shoved it at me between my arm and waist.

"And take your mattress with you, in case you're tired and want to sleep!" He smirked at me with contempt to show me how satisfied he was with himself for finding a way to get back at me. I dragged the mattress with me, opened the door and left. Despite the fact that I already knew it, I was still struck by how insignificant I was to him… stupid old man, I thought to myself furiously, I'll find some other arrangement.

I dragged the mattress with me down the hall, just like when we were moving, but at the same time I was afraid, because I knew that now I was alone.

CHAPTER 5

Daniel

I moved to my right, hugging wall. The sounds grew louder around me. It seemed that shadows flickered across my face over and over, but I didn't change direction and I kept moving slowly along the wall, step by step. Now I heard whispers, and again saw a silhouette cross my face. The thought entered my mind that the best defense is attack. I kept walking to the right, waiting patiently until I heard a sound in front of me, and without thinking, I leaned over and reached out. I grabbed what seemed to be a leg, and then I felt a whole body fall and hit the ground. Again, I heard footsteps. There were at least three of us there…

The leg I was holding did not move for a few moments, and then suddenly it started shaking wildly, trying to get out of my grip, so I leaped on it and grabbed the whole body, my arm across its chest. I held on as hard as I could, not to let it get away. The light came back on suddenly. I made out a figure about two meters away, holding a flashlight.

They were two of them now. One was wearing a leather cap holding the flashlight in his hand, standing near what seemed to be another entrance to a tunnel, and the other one was held tight in my grip. I saw how gaunt and skinny the boy was; he was just skin and bones. Again, he tried to break free of my hold on him.

The boy standing at the other entrance shouted: "Let him go, and I'll let you go back, or else I'll call the rest of the guys and you'll never get out of here!"

"You want me to let him go? Give me back the bag you stole from my girlfriend!"

"We didn't take any bag, leave him alone!"

I looked again at the boy I was holding and saw his frightened look. I relaxed my grip and the boy ran straight toward his friend. I started to go in their direction, but in a second, the light was gone and the boys had disappeared in the darkness. I wanted to go after them, but I knew I had better head back to the concert hall, because the intermission must have ended. I turned back into the tunnel. The battle was lost, perhaps, but not the war.

I crawled back through the tunnel. The opening was shut tight, and I needed to open it, this time from inside. I don't know why, but I made sure close it up tight so no one would notice it. I quickly dusted off my clothes and went to the corridor, up the stairs, and back to the hall where the performance was in progress. I groped my way to row twelve, and saw my father's questioning hand raised in my direction. I said "S'cuse me" to a dozen or so people, and kept going towards my seat until I finally rejoined the rest of the family.

"Everything all right?" Catia asked me.

"Everything's fine." I tried to act normal even though I was still agitated, but I didn't want them to know. No yet. I couldn't concentrate during the concert and afterwards. I kept thinking about what I had just been through. Then the show ended, everyone applauded and started leaving. When we passed the bulletin board on the way out, I stopped for a moment to see when the next show was scheduled.

It was in two more days, on Tuesday. I don't remember what show it was, I just wanted to know when I could roam around the Athenaeum again...

On Tuesday, I was there early. It was twenty minutes after seven and the Athenaeum had just opened its doors. I brought with me a little flashlight in my bag. I headed toward the bathroom. I was the only one there, but it was not the first time I had been early for a show, so I knew I could walk around freely. Sometimes I would come when the doors opened and watch the final preparations before the performance.

I reached the entrance and quickly began to remove its cover. I was careful not to make any noise. I crawled in, and just before I closed the paneland was in total darkness, I pulled the flashlight out of my bag and turned it on. Now I could see where I was. After crawling through the tunnel, I reached the open area where I had encountered the two boys. It was a space about five meters long and three meters wide. The ceiling was at least three meters high. The floor and walls were made of dirt overlaid with little stones. I approached the other entrance, where I had seen the boys before they disappeared. It turned out to be an opening into another tunnel, this time an even bigger one, about one and a half meters wide. I had to crouch down to go through it, and I began walking hunched over, holding the flashlight.

The tunnel was partially made of concrete, while other parts were from the same mixture of dirt and stone, as was the large space before it. It seemed there was unfinished construction there, maybe with the intention of making a drainage canal. Only after walking in a half crouch about thirty meters did I see a connection to yet another hall, and from it came a faint light. I turned off my flashlight so the light wouldn't be noticed on the other side. As I moved slowly towards the end of the tunnel, what I saw amazed me...

It was an enormously wide, round hall, with walls about ten meters high. In front of me, about 40 meters, were stone walls with indentations that looked like small caves, each with three openings set at equal distances. Some of them had half-built staircases with steps too smooth and a slope that seemed too steep to climb. There were two caves on the second floor and three on the first. The openings were decorated with murals. Some were unfinished and others elaborated and impressive. Most of the paintings were black, but some of them had colors such as red, blue, yellow and green. One of the caves had a painting of the sun and rolling hills on the left side and the moon and stars on the right. The paintings joined at the bottom of the tunnel opening where the words "The Fortress knights" were spelled out with crisscross markings, each in a different style. I saw sheets stretched underneath and between the caves, colored blankets sticking out, and stretched rope with ragged clothes hung on them. I backed away quickly into the tunnel so no one would see me, and carefully looked up at the ceiling. It was concave in the shape of a dome with a round opening covered with murky glass, and through it came the faint light by which I was able to see.

Suddenly I saw two heads sticking out at the mouth of the cave on the second floor, which led to a relatively complete staircase. They noticed me. It was too late to hide.

I came out of the tunnel and walked slowly across the floor. All at once, there was a shout from two boys who had seen me.

"Matei, Matei! There's an intruder in The Fortress!" They

shouted towards the first floor. Older boys and younger children in ragged clothes began to emerge from the decorated caves one by one. The first three boys, all of them with wild black hair and about the same height, came out and started moving towards me. After them, a slightly smaller boy appeared, with blond hair and wearing glasses, and he in turn was followed by the boy wearing the cap. I recognized them. They were the two boys who took Catia's purse.

Finally, the two children who had seen me came out, the youngest of them all, both of them with reddish hair. They all formed a line, about twenty meters from me, and stood there silently. They were waiting for something, or rather, for someone... The last one emerged from the largest cave on the first floor. Above the entrance to this cave was the inscription "The commander's room" and had murals of swords from each side. He was the only one who had to bend over when he came out. He was the tallest and most solidly built. He had short, light brown hair, and walked slowly towards me, step by step, with a staff too short for walking, but long enough to hit. His brown eyes never left me for a second. He stopped and stood between me and the line of children.

"You are in our fortress; uninvited guests are not welcome here."

"I know it's your place, and I also know its secret. I promise not to tell anyone. I didn't come to hurt anyone. I'm just asking for what you took from my friend a week ago, a white bag, it's very important to me. If you give it back to me, I won't bother you anymore."

Silence. Our eyes met, but no one moved. The tall boy turned to the three black-haired children and laughed.

"I'll find you your white bag," the laughter was quickly replaced with a deadly serious expression, "but I don't want to see you here ever again. Is that clear?"

I nodded in agreement.

The boy with glasses shouted, "I'll go look for it," and ran into one of the caves. A few minutes later he came out carrying the bag, went down the stairs, and gave the bag to the tall boy with the staff, then returned to his place in line.

The tall boy, who had not looked away from me all that time, moved toward me and stopped right in front of me. He looked at me silently, perhaps because he wanted to watch me carefully, or maybe to make me feel threatened. Only after about thirty seconds, he handed me the bag. I took it and nodded thank-you and reached into my pocket to pull some candies I had.

"For you," I said.

One of the black-haired children approached me, and only then did I notice she was a girl. She quickly took the candy from my hand as if afraid that if she didn't, I would put it back in my pocket. The children all stood in line, as I turned and started to go back into the tunnel I had come from.

As I walked, I heard the tall boy shout at me: "You brought four candies for eight people! Are we supposed to cut them in half?! We don't want your candy! Don't come back here anymore!"

I kept walking without a word or even turning around. Only when I was back in the tunnel did I look back, from my crouching position. The children had already returned to their caves. I continued bent over and entered the smaller tunnel. I crept into it and carefully let myself out to the bathroom, making sure no one was there to see. I ought to have been satisfied that I did not give up and was able to return Catia's purse that seemed to be lost forever, but I didn't feel happy. I felt that I should have stayed. I felt a longing to return... Only when I left the bathroom did I look in the bag. It was empty.

Disappointed, I continued to Catia's house. I was sorry I'd be giving her back an empty bag, but I thought she still might find comfort in it. Her mother opened the door, and her surprised look immediately changed to one more serious, hinting to me that a late hour visit without advance notice is received with suspicion. I went to Catia and somewhat sadly gave her the bag. I thought she would be so disappointed to find out the bag was empty, but instead she opened it and her fingers went towards a hidden side pocket in the bag, which I had never known existed. She began gently pulling out her pretty handkerchief. It was a wonderful surprise for both of us.

When you find something precious to you that you thought was lost forever, a light comes on inside you, which makes you believe everything happens for a reason. That is the light I saw in Catia's face, and that made the adventure all worthwhile. I was so happy that evening that I forgot everything that had happened, but I knew I would go back to The Fortress one day; if only I knew then, under what circumstances...

***

Everything returned to normal afterwards. I tried to keep going with my regular activities, going to school, hanging out with Ion, Andrei and Lucian, passing time with Catia and the family, but I could not stop thinking about The Fortress and the kids. One day, on my way home from school, I went to the kiosk and bought a bag full of all the candy I could with the money I had. That evening I returned to the Athenaeum, went through the bathroom and tunnels and arrived again at The Fortress. I walked to the middle of the hall and stopped.

No one came out to meet me.

"Hello! Anybody here?"

The tall boy with the staff was the first to come out of the cave. He looked at me.

"You! What are you doing here?" The other children began to appear behind him.

"Sorry, I didn't come to bother you, I wanted to bring you candies, nothing more, and see that everything is fine, or that maybe you need something."

I pulled the bag of candy out and the kids rushed at me. I saw how angry the tall boy was, but he didn't say a word. When each of the children had candy in his mouth or was bargaining for candy with another child, the tall boy spoke again.

"Everything was fine here; it was fine before you came. You gave your candy, now go."

I turned and walked away. Suddenly a voice broke the silence.

"Thank you" echoed in the cave. I turned to see who it had come from. It was the boy with the cap. I smiled and walked on.

From that day on, I would occasionally arrive with a bag of candy or bread and cheese or anything I could put in a bag without anyone noticing. The tall boy with the staff would look at me menacingly, but did not say a word. I was bringing a commodity he could not refuse - food.

I began to know the children. First their names then the caves in which they slept and lived, and gradually all their personal histories.

Nicu (Niculai) and Doru, who had wild black hair, were

brothers. Nicu was two years older than his brother, but they were the same height. They were the oldest of the children, and hung around with Rita, a girl their age. She also had black hair, a little longer and fuller than the two boys' hair. At first, I assumed she was their sister, but I discovered that they became a trio only after Nicu and Doru had arrived at The Fortress. All three were born in Bucharest, street children. Rita began roaming around the city squares more and more, until her aunt threw her out of the house, and she lived on the streets. In a while, she became friendly with Nicu and Doru, and they had become inseparable ever since.

The boy with the blond hair and glasses who hung around with Nelu was called Dumitru, but everyone called him Mitu. The frame of his glasses was covered with bandaged patches to keep it from breaking to pieces, and his glasses were so cracked I wondered how he could see anything.

The youngest were a pair of brothers, red-headed like my sister Lili. They were smaller than everyone else, and looked alike. They said they were a year apart, but I was sure they were twins. Their names were Lizica and Dinu.

Finally, there was Matei. He was biggest of all, the only one who looked like an adult, and was about my age. He was also one of the street kids. Nicu, Doru and Rita had begun roaming the streets with him since he always found a way to get them money or food. One freezing winter day, Matei, Nicu, Doru and Rita entered the Athenaeum to take shelter from the cold. They hid in the bathroom until the show ended and the crowd left the hall. They were sure it was safe to come out, but then they saw one of the guards patrolling near the staircase. Afraid they would be discovered, they ran back to the bathroom and started to look for a way out, until Matei came across the wooden board, and the rest was history. They had their own little kingdom and no one could bother them there. They found an easy way in and out of the building without having to pass through the main doors, so they brought with them everything they had, and made it their home. It protected them and they protected it. That's how Matei gave it its name: The Fortress.

Matei was the undisputed leader of the group. You could see it in the other children's behavior towards him. Everything needed his approval.

Despite the fact that I did not like the implied threat of his staff, I still respected him. After all, the children around him were his responsibility, and he saw to it that they had food and shelter, and that was undeniable.

I knew from the looks he gave me that my presence threatened him, but even he could not refuse the food I brought for them every time I came to visit. Luckily, he became accustomed to my visits there, and slowly, once he saw my presence didn't undermine his authority, he stopped glaring at me with a threatening look. I came to know this cohesive group of children, each of whom came from a reality much harsher than I had ever known. That was precisely what drew me to The Fortress - to learn about their reality. These children were under the magic spell of The Fortress and I in turn, had fallen under their spell.

Of all of them, I liked Nelu best. He was different from the others: going around in his brown trousers, beige shirt with the white buttons and red stripe trim on the edges. The brown cap always on his head. There was something in his manner and way of speaking that conveyed a calm that did not suit his young age. More than that, it did not fit the reality in which he lived. Often, when I spoke to him, I would forget that he was not a classmate of mine, but a child whose main concern was how to survive the next day. Yet, I never heard him complain.

I learned a lot from Nelu about the children's way of life. They would divide up into pairs every day, and their task was to leave The Fortress and come back with loot. The loot could be leftovers from bakeries, kiosks, butcher shops, stalls in the market... some found, some stolen. From time to time, they would come back with a purse or a bag they had pinched. Any coins they found were important. All the spoils would reach the great cave, the "home base", as they called it, where they would divide everything evenly under the scrutiny of Matei. The main hall was the place for everyone to meet. This band of children could serve as an example for many adults in the way they conducted themselves.

The cave on the ground floor, opposite the entrance to the hall, was Matei's cave. He was the only one who slept in his own cave. On the right was a smaller cave where Nicu, Doru and Rita slept, on the left, the "home base". Above them, on the second floor, were two even smaller caves. On the left, the cave where Mitu and Nelu slept and, on the right, the cave of Lizica and Dinu.

At night, after Doru was sent to make sure that the last worker had left the Athenaeum, and they could go out, the children went into the bathroom, and filled buckets of water from the faucets there. Twice a week they went two by two, to take showers in the locker rooms. One day I was with the children in The Fortress and sat down to talk to Nelu. It was already eight-thirty at night.

After ten minutes of conversation, he said to me, "Come with me, I have something you might want to see." I hesitated.

I didn't want to do anything that would lead to a confrontation with Matei.

"Don't you have to ask Matei? … I mean…"

"Don't worry."

Nelu led me to the third floor. It was the first time I had gone up there, it was by way of a crumbling staircase. It wasn't clear if the stairs had deteriorated over the years, or if their construction had never been completed. There were several apertures in the wall, most of them did not lead to a cave as on the lower floors, but were large indentations in the wall. We entered the second aperture on the left. On the right side of it was an opening no more than half a meter high. Nelu started to crawl through and signaled me to follow. I dragged myself after him three or four meters.

"Don't worry, we're almost there!"

We got through the crevice and stood up. We were in a dark room. On the opposite wall was a spectacular view of dozens of glowing dots.

"Where are we?"

Nelu pressed his finger to his lips for me to be quiet and come nearer to the glowing dots.

"It's starting right now!"

Only when I got closer did I realize that Nelu was not looking at the dots, but through them. Their glow was from light coming in. I looked through one of the dots and the wonder was revealed… It was the magnificent Hall of the Athenaeum. The stage was right in front of my eyes, these were holes, through which you could see the entire hall.

Within a few moments, the lights in the hall dimmed and the stage lights came on. I realized that the wall was behind all the seats, directly in front of the stage so that it could be seen clearly through the holes. On the stage were all the members of the Philharmonic Orchestra. I could actually identify some of them, and with the wave of the conductor's arm, they began to play.

I was in a dark, dust-filled cave watching the orchestra of the Bucharest Philharmonic performing Beethoven's Symphony No. 8 through a slit in the wall! It was the most special performance I had ever seen. After about twenty minutes of listening to the music of the violins, the cello, the flutes and the clarinets, I told Nelu that I had to go home, or they would start wondering where I was.

Nelu continued watching through one of the slits.

"It's funny; I just remembered it's my birthday today."

"Your birthday, Nelu? Really?"

"Really." he said this with his head bowed.

I hadn't understood before this the meaning of being all alone in the world. The room was dark, but in the glimmer of light coming from the stage, I was sure I saw tears streaming down Nelu's cheek. I stayed with him until the end of the performance because I knew that nothing else mattered at that moment except Nelu's loneliness. I didn't want him to feel completely by himself. At least on that birthday, Nelu was not alone in the world.

Since that day, my visits to the Athenaeum became more frequent. Sometimes I would stay for hours, talking to Nelu. I told them at home that I was just looking around the Athenaeum, which I had often done before, so no one suspected anything.

I gradually got to know Nelu really well. It began when I asked about the cap he always wore. Nelu said that the cap was a constant reminder that he had to go back for his sister and his mother. He had been living in The Fortress for more than a year, finding refuge a little bit after he ran away. Mitu, who had arrived just a few months before, introduced him to The Fortress. Nelu told me that Doru and Nicu had been there for more than two years, and that one day, a few months ago, Matei had brought Lizica and Dinu there, after finding them living on the street. It was the first time I thought that Matei did not have a heart of stone.

The children all lived under Matei's stern rules. The day began early. They would split into groups, hurry out of the caves and out to the street through the staircase window before anyone saw them, and then they would spend the whole day trying to find something they could bring back to the Athenaeum. Nicu, Doru and Rita were one team, Mitu and Nelu were another, and Matei, Lizica and Dinu were team three.

They could use the bathroom in the Athenaeum, but they had to go there only in pairs, always in total silence, and never during the opening hours of the place. From time to time, the children fought with each other, but it was enough for the menacing appearance of Matei with the staff in his hand for them to stop. So it was that I discovered the secrets that made it possible for the children to live in The Fortress for so long without anybody noticing them.

Descending from the bathroom to the Athenaeum maintenance floor, in the middle of the stairs, was a small window. Only the maintenance workers used the staircase, and they didn't notice that although the window looked like it was closed; it could still be opened from the other side.

The days stretched into weeks and the weeks into months. Perhaps it is the way of the world but, as time went by, my stay in the Athenaeum with the street children was more and more pleasing to me as the outside world began to crumble. Romania's situation deteriorated each day. Eighty percent of the population lived in rural areas. It had become a backward country with an unstable economy, fertile ground for extreme right-wing movements such as the *Garda de Fier*[8], which toughened the laws and attitude toward minorities, especially Jews.

It started with little things. One day my sister came back from school saying that some of the girls had harassed her and called her "dirty Jew." I was also called that more than once when we were playing soccer in the schoolyard. It was in the air, but we chose to ignore the hostility. I remember another time when I went with my mother to pick up Lili from school. The mother of one of the children looked at Lili's red hair and said to my mother: "Another Jewish brat?" I saw how hard it was for my mother to control herself, but she said nothing. Soon, with the backing of the Garda de Fier, hooligans ransacked the Great Synagogue and Jewish businesses. They broke showcases, smeared display windows with Jewish stars and scribbled "Jew" everywhere, and stopped customers from entering. It was impossible to ignore. We painted the mezuzah on the side of the door of our house in brown, the color of the doorpost, so it wouldn't stand out.

Then came my father's letter of dismissal. At first we didn't know, because he made sure to be out of the house during working hours, and then he started being absent even after working hours and would arrive home late at night. One night I complained to him that he was never home, that he had

8   Romanian anti-Semitic fascist movement

forgotten all about us. He didn't say anything and moved away. I wanted to shout at him but my mother took me aside and explained to me, out of earshot, that after he had been fired he started working two shifts at the butcher shop and was simply exhausted.

I will never forget my parents' faces as they sat in the living room listening to the radio and heard that Germany, led by Hitler, had invaded and conquered Czechoslovakia. By this time, my parents were very afraid. They could not hide their fear from us, though they tried as hard as they could to pretend to be calm in front of us.

Whether it was King Carol II of Romania, the Garda de Fier, or Antonescu, ruler of Romania, the general directive was to be rid of the Jewish population, and the difficult situation was felt more and more, as time went on.

Bread, which had already been a rare commodity in Bucharest, became even harder to obtain. We were thankful for each morsel, even if it was a week old, and we began to forget what fresh bread even tasted like. In those days, we went to school with bread that my mother had soaked in a little sugar to make it taste better. My sister, who did not like sweets, took her bread seasoned with oil and a little salt. It was hard to get used to all this, but we didn't complain because we saw how troubled our parents were.

One day Catia and I lay on the lawn in the park, talking together, looking up at the clouds.

"Do you remember the house we went to once, Daniel?"

"What house?"

"The one on the outskirts of Bucharest, the one we rode our bikes for an hour and a half to get to."

"The house your parents built next to their friends?"

"Yes."

"If anything should happen, you should know we'll be there."

"What do you mean if anything should happen?" Catia was always elegant and smiling, so I was startled by her worried tone of voice.

"Just remember, we'll be there." She said and immediately got up and got on her bike, with me following.

As time went on, I was able bring fewer and fewer treats with me on my visits to the children at The Fortress, until finally I could bring no more. I hoped no one would ask me why.

One day, the youngest one, Dinu, stopped me.

"Daniel, why aren't you bringing us anything good to eat anymore?"

I was ashamed to tell him the truth and couldn't think of a word to say. My mouth opened, but nothing came out. Suddenly Nelu suddenly intervened.

"That's funny, Daniel and I were just talking about that, and he told me he was going to bring you something very soon."

I looked at Nelu questioningly.

On one hand, I was relieved that he had gotten me off the hook, but I wondered how I would keep the promise Nelu had just made to Dinu.

"Really?!" said Dinu. Nelu nodded and Dinu went back in the cave.

"First," said Nelu, coming over to me - raising his hand and pressing it against my chin – "you can close your mouth, so no fly gets in. Second, don't worry and follow me." Nelu led me out of the Athenaeum. We walked a few blocks and stopped.

"What are we doing here?"

"Look to your right," he said. "What do you see?" I saw the

Great Church, one of the oldest in Bucharest.

"What, the Church?"

"Yes."

I looked at him with puzzlement.

"Do you want us to pray?"

Nelu smiled at me, "I don't think you understand. Do you see the cars parked outside the church?"

"Yes."

"See the people waiting outside?"

"Yes."

"There's a couple getting married."

"Do you know them, Nelu? You want us to go and congratulate them?"

He laughed, "No, that's not what I meant." He took my arm.

"Come on, they'll be coming out at any moment. Everyone will be busy with the couple and they won't notice us."

Before I realized what was happening, we were in the church square together with the crowd who began to cheer the couple coming out and going down the stairs. Nelu pulled at my arm.

"You know what they're throwing at the couple?"

"What they always throw at newly married couples?"

"Candies!"

Just then, the candy started flying in all directions.

"Fill your pockets with everything you can!"

Like two highly efficient cleaners, we scooped up lots of candy. We pulled out our shirts and made them into big pockets that were quickly filled with the candy. We had stuffed so much candy in them we had trouble walking back to the Athenaeum, and I'm sure we left a candy trail behind us...

As we entered The Fortress, Dinu ran toward me and stopped.

He looked at our pockets and saw they were stuffed with candies.

"All this... for me... I mean, for us?!"

Without a word, I stuck my hand in my shirt and pulled out a handful of candies for Dinu. Then Nelu and I gave candies out to each of the children, under the watchful eye of Matei. Nelu and I stood watching the children, as they all happily chomped away on their candy.

"I don't know how you did it, Nelu, but thanks... it's just... I..."

I wanted to explain to Nelu that these were hard times, and that for a while now there was almost nothing to eat, but the words didn't come out and Nelu interrupted.

"Don't you know how many candies you already brought us? I just paid off the debt to you, so shut up, you look like a dummy."

We both started laughing. I couldn't stop, partly because Nelu's laugh was so contagious, but also because I felt so relieved. It had been a long time since I had laughed that way.

CHAPTER 6

War on the Horizon

On January 21, 1941, the Legionnaires' Rebellion erupted. Word spread through the neighborhood of what was to come - within a few days an angry mob would fill the streets of Bucharest. I still remember the night the riots started. It was terrifying because the first to feel the rage of the mob were the minorities. My father always told us that if we hear commotion in the street, we need to close all the windows and move away from them. One night that was not enough to keep safe: the night the mob attacked our house.

The crowd began attacking the neighborhoods of Văcărești and Dudești, as well as our own neighborhood, bearing down on the houses and buildings. We saw people dragged from their homes screaming, their houses in flame. We did not know what to do. In our worst imaginings, we never dreamed the war would come right to our doorstep.

Lili and I looked out for a moment from the living room window and saw pieces of broken furniture all over the street. We saw people being hauled outside by force, windows were shattered, just before my father pulled us away and gestured for us to be quiet and stay crouched in a corner, far from the window. The shouting was getting nearer. The broken glass, the people screaming, tore at our hearts. My father grabbed my hand and signaled us to go into the bedroom. But it was too late…

A rock smashed through the living room as we were walking towards the bedroom. It shattered the glass into jagged bits.

The rock landed close to Lili, and my mother quickly moved her away to the far right side of the room while my father and I went to the left corner of the room.

We didn't dare raise our heads, hoping that the rock had been thrown due to all the commotion outside and not deliberately aimed at our house.

We heard shouting: "Look over there!" "Found another damn Jew!" Shut her up!"

The roaring of the crowd and the screams of the victims grew stronger. Suddenly a big, hairy arm opened the window frame and emerged from the shattered window, followed by a large dirty head. A rough, bristly face gradually took form in front of us. He looked to the right and saw my mother and sister. He gaped at them and smiled.

"*Cele mai frumoase fete mai mai!*"[9] he sang as he gawked at them and continued pushing himself through the window. My mother and sister were terrified. For the first time in my life, I saw evil wearing a smile.

He continued to pull himself through the window. His hairy arm was about to touch the floor. He kept his eyes on my mother and sister as he pulled in his big belly to get himself in through the window. One hand was now resting on the floor, and he began to pull himself inside the house. His eyes squinted, searching for something he could get a

---

9 *Cele mai frumoase fete mai mai*! – Ah, such beautiful girls!

grip on. Suddenly, I caught sight of the paperweight. Usually it was on the bookshelf, but now it was lying on the floor. The paperweight was a cannon-shaped piece of iron that my grandfather had made for my father. It was one of my father's most beloved possessions. I jumped up and grabbed the weight in my hand. The large hairy thing that had penetrated our house still did not notice my father and me on the other side of the window. I moved towards him quietly. He was so focused on my mother and sister, he didn't see me.

I was holding the paperweight so tightly the metal seemed to bore holes in my palm. I raised my arm, and with all the strength of my fifteen years, I bashed him in his head.

He fell - his head on the carpet and his feet on the windowsill. My father quickly pulled his bulk inside.

"Andrei!" There were shouts from outside, "Andrei!" However, they were swallowed up by the yelling and shrieking all around.

I fell to the floor. A red stain had begun to form around the man's head, spreading on the carpet.

"Everybody all right?" I yelled.

"We gave that ape what he deserved! We did…" My father grabbed my arm. "Capul plecat sabia nu taie[10]. Help me hide him. Quickly!"

We maneuvered the body onto the carpet and got it to the corner of the living room. My father took Lili and me aside.

"You and your sister, each of you take your school bags and throw in all the things you can! Whatever you can manage to stuff in there - a pair of shoes, your favorite clothes, underwear, socks!"

---

10   *Capul plecat sabia nu taie* = No sword cuts off a bowed head.

"Constantin," my mother stopped him, "you are scaring the children."

"Clara, this is not the time for discussion, we are leaving now before the second wave comes, and it will come, and they'll look for this baboon who was with them. We are leaving, and I don't know for how long." There was utter silence in the room. "Come on! As quick as you can!" We did as my father said and packed quickly. There was no time to think about what to take and what to leave. The bag my mother had prepared had come open, and she fell to the floor weeping. My father picked her up, hugged her and said, "Clara, we'll get through this." My mother's head was still drooping, my father holding her by the shoulders.

Look at me. My mother lifted her head. "Have I ever lied to you? We'll get through this." She nodded her head and quickly started packing the bag.

"Only dark colors, so we won't stand out, hurry!" Ten minutes later, we were ready to leave.

"Put your coats on and cover your heads."

We opened the door of the house and ran quickly down the corridor to the back entrance of the building. My father went first, and when he saw that the way was clear, he signaled us to join him. Before we understood the significance of what was happening, we were already out on the street. My father led us through the alleys, and my mother was behind us. They acted as a team to protect us.

"Where are we going Constantin?" My mother asked, in a throaty whisper.

"It's not safe here anymore, we'll go south, and I know somewhere we..." my father replied.

"Constantin! Did you see that mob?! It's not safe outside!

We should have stayed at home, at least we could have gone on hiding there."

"We cannot return Clara, we cannot go back..."

Before my mother could answer, I grabbed my father's sleeve.

"You're right, Dad, but Mom is right too, we can't go home, but we can't wander like this in the streets, they're probably searching for us already. It's too dangerous."

"I know Daniel, but don't worry, just promise me you'll look after your sister," and he turned away.

"Father!"

"Take care of your sister Daniel, she's terrified."

"Please! Listen to me for a minute!" I almost screamed at him. My father finally turned to me.

"What is it Daniel, for God's sake?!"

"Dad, I know where we can hide."

"Daniel, I know you want to help, but leave it to me."

"Dad, wherever you go, it won't be safe, look at me, I know where to take us."

"Daniel, I do not think this is the place for..."

"Dad, if ever in my life I should have your trust, it's now!"

My father looked at me curiously and went silent for a moment. He found it hard to believe there was any other possibility except to try to get to his friends.

"Dad, listen to me, I don't know where you want to take us, but the place I know is just ten minutes away, and we have to get off the streets as soon as we can."

My father paused for a few seconds and then opened his mouth. I thought he was going to scold me.

"Lead the way, son," he said.

I could find my way to the Athenaeum with my eyes closed, so in a few minutes we were there.

"Here? Are you mad? You think we'll be safe here?"

"Wait, father, this is nothing, wait till you see."

Shouts were not far off, the mob was still close and the only choice was to go ahead with my plan. We quickly ran round the Athenaeum and reached the window above the maintenance floor staircase. I opened it and helped my mother and sister in, then my father and I followed.

"Daniel, they can easily track us down here, I'm not sure it's a good idea."

"Dad, believe me, we've just started."

We continued up the stairs toward the bathroom. I removed the wooden board, and they all stood stunned at the sight of the narrow tunnel that had been revealed behind it.

"We'll have to crawl a little, but it's not far."

We made our way through the tunnel into the dark space and from there to the second tunnel until we were in front of The Fortress. They stopped and stared in amazement at what they saw.

"Ladies and gentlemen," I said, "welcome to The Fortress."

CHAPTER 7

Nelu

I remember the day they appeared in the hall. It seems like only yesterday. Clara, Constantin, Lili, and Daniel. We all had heard them and gathered in the hall. I remember we approached them and formed the line according to Matei's orders. There was a sudden muted storm of silence, an instant when the eyes saw everything and searched for a way to react. No one really knew what to do.

It was frightening, of course, but I knew that if these people had come with Daniel, they were all right. I knew he would not have betrayed us. When I looked at them standing there helplessly with their bags, I knew something bad had happened. I understood that they had come to stay.

"Who are these people?" Matei approached Daniel angrily.

"My family, I had no choice. I brought them because they broke into our house; we have nowhere else to go."

"And how long are they going to be here?"

"Until we can find a way to go on from here."

It was clear that Daniel was tense and nervous. Fortunately, he managed to keep the conversation calm to avoid a flare-up.

"I know I may be asking a lot, and maybe you think I don't deserve it, but if you can help me and accept my family, as you have accepted me, I promise we will do everything to keep you from being disturbed."

"If you want to stay here, you will have to do your share just like everyone else." said Matei. He was the only one to speak in these cases, especially with all the children around him, watching.

"Of course," said Daniel.

Daniel's father turned to him and said, "Daniel, all these caves, these drawings, do they… live here?"

"There's something I didn't tell you… Do you remember the day that Catia's purse was stolen? Well… that's the day I found this…"

Everyone was still standing around open-mouthed. The other children came closer to get a look at the new guests. Except for Daniel, there had never been any guests in The Fortress in all the time the children had been there.

Matei motioned with his head for Daniel to follow him, and Daniel gestured to his family to join him. They passed by the rest of us and Daniel looked at me. There was something upsetting in his eyes, something I had never seen before. I looked at all their frightened looks as they passed by me. His little sister held her mother's hand, and carried a bag in her other hand that was almost as big as she was. The blonde woman, whose hair was somewhat ruffled, some of it bound with a rubber band, moved cautiously, and the father in the black suit looked all around, scrutinizing the entire area. The three of them, looking apprehensive, followed behind Daniel and Matei.

Matei led them to one of the caves on the third level, almost the only one that could be accessed on that floor, except for my secret cave, from where Daniel and I had watched the performance in the concert hall.

"Don't worry, Matei, they won't be any trouble, I'll take care of it," I said.

He looked at me for a moment and went on to his cave. I knew he did not like the whole idea. I followed him quickly, and before Matei had time to say anything, I pulled out some white blankets that were still with the loot and had not been distributed. I also took with me two bricks we'd gathered from when they renovated the foyer area in the Athenaeum.

I took the blankets and bricks and went up to the cave where the family had entered and stood at the entrance.

"This is what I've managed for now, so you'll have something at least to sit on and cover yourselves with. There's not much light in here now, but in the morning we'll be able to make some order in here."

I turned to go. I knew they were uncomfortable, so I did not want to disturb too much. Daniel took my hand.

"Thanks, Nelu."

I smiled at him. "Don't worry," I said. "You're in good hands."

CHAPTER 8

Daniel

My father was the first to come to himself and opened his mouth.

"All these caves, these drawings, do they live in here?"

"Yes, this is the most protected place we can be in."

We stood there, each with his bag in his hand in front of the approaching children, and didn't say a word.

The children came closer and stood a meter from us. They looked at us curiously.

Matei approached us, and without looking at my parents, asked, "Who are these people?"

"My family," I replied. "I had no choice, I brought them here because the rioters broke into our house, and we have nowhere else to go."

"How long are they going to be here?"

"Until we find somewhere to continue on to from here," I answered patiently, biting my tongue. I knew how important the hierarchy was to him that everyone should know who was in charge. "Maybe I'm asking for a lot, maybe you think I do not deserve it," I said, looking at all the children, "but if you can help us and accept them like you accepted me—

Matei interrupted: "They will have to do their share just like everyone here."

"Of course."

After a long pause, Matei motioned for me to follow him. I did so, trying to look calm and in control, but the truth is my legs felt like rubber. All the fury and commotion we had been through had begun to wear on me. All I wanted was to find a quiet corner and close my eyes.

Matei led us through the stairs to a deserted cave on the third floor. He gestured for us to enter, and without another word, he turned and went back to his cave.

Nelu went up to him and whispered something in his ear, then turned toward Matei's cave and disappeared into it.

I entered our cave with my family. Except for the dirt and stones, there was nothing but darkness.

"So this is where you went to all those times?" Asked my father. "I had a feeling you were up to something," he said, putting his hand on my shoulder, a half smile on his face. "It's lucky I've got a son with some tricks up his sleeve!"

My mother and Lili began unpacking the bags. I saw the fear in their eyes and my heart ached for them. I couldn't tell if it was because of what we were going through or what we were going to have to go through. Our lives were shattered. Nothing was sure anymore.

Nelu came into the cave with two blankets and two bricks.

"This is what I've managed so far, so at least you'll have something to sit on and cover yourselves with. There's not much light in here now, but in the morning we'll be able to make some order here," he said, pausing to look at the bags we had brought. He looked at my family. "I'm Nelu, by the way, welcome."

As Nelu turned to leave, I walked toward the exit from the

cave, grabbed his hand and thanked him.

I went back into the cave and all of us got down on the blankets we had spread out. I lay my head on the blanket. I was exhausted, anxious and frightened, and yet one thought kept echoing in my head before I fell asleep. What had happened to Catia?

The first few days were hard, and getting used to the new reality wasn't easy. The other children were very curious, but they were afraid to come near us so as not to anger Matei who continued to see us as intruders. The only one who dared to sit with us sometimes was Nelu, and he heard from us what had brought us to the Athenaeum…

For the next few days, hearing in the background the noise of the shouting, shooting, and glass being smashed on the streets, we didn't dare to venture outside the hall. We survived on the scraps of food we had brought with us and the buckets of water the children brought us from the taps in the bathroom. We had to wait for night to go to the bathroom. It wasn't safe to go there during the day. After several days, Matei sent Nicu to check what was happening outside the Athenaeum. Nicu was his first choice because he was the oldest, but more than that, he was also the fastest and the most likely to come back in one piece.

Nicu returned after half an hour, panting and frightened. He told us things that were hard to hear: bodies lying bruised and naked in the street, clothes and objects thrown everywhere, battered people in torn clothes led away by uniformed men; he told of an inflamed mob cursing and yelling "Dirty Jews" at the people being led through the streets, with others standing by and watching, doing nothing.

It was hard for us to believe that this was the same Bucharest we loved so much. It had become a hell.

A few more days passed before the shouting and shooting stopped. It was a window of opportunity to replenish the stock of food that was running out. Matei sent Nicu, Doru, Nelu, and Mitu. I wanted to join them, but Nelu grabbed me and dragged me aside.

"It's too dangerous for you to go out, maybe they're still looking for you." He was right; it wasn't safe yet in the streets.

My sister Lili couldn't sleep at night. I sat by her in the darkness and told her stories of beautiful princesses, brave knights and fierce dragons, and for a moment it seemed I was telling her stories while she was at home in her bed, and we forgot we were lying in a dark cave. Finally, Lili would fall asleep and I would fall asleep just seconds after.

One night I told Lili about the constellations in the sky. She liked to hear about them. Once, I saw Lizica and Dinu poking their heads in at the entrance to the cave as if trying to listen, but afraid to enter.

"Come on in, I'm just telling the story of the constellation Pegasus, do you know it?"

"No."

I took a small stone and sketched the alignment of the stars on the dirt floor. I tried to draw the shape of a horse as best as I could.

"This is Pegasus, a winged horse, the son of Medusa and Poseidon, who fought many battles, but when Bellerophon wanted to ride Pegasus to Mount Olympus, Pegasus refused and flew there alone. And there he sits among the stars to this day."

"Is he really up there in the sky?" asked Dinu.

"Really, and you know what, we too will one day be as free

as he is in the starry sky, and I will show him to you." The days stretched into a week, the week became a month, and we still could not go out.

One day we sat in the cave after having eaten two tomatoes Nicu and Doru had brought us. The children outside were quarreling over some candies under Matei's menacing gaze, and I was helping Lili build a tower from a pack of cards Lizica had brought her. Suddenly, my father leaned toward me, touched my shoulder and motioned me to be quiet. There was a sparkle in his eyes.

"What is it?"

"Listen, just listen."

I nodded to my father that I didn't understand.

"Ignore the children shouting for a moment, and listen carefully," he said.

It took a few seconds more before I could focus, but then suddenly I heard what my father wanted me to hear.

A soft, barely audible sound reverberated from the walls of The Fortress.

At first, piano, and then violins and cellos... The sound seemed so far away, but still it was warm and familiar. My father went outside the cave and gathered the squabbling children together. He motioned them to calm down and listen.

Slowly they began to hear... and to listen.

"Do you know what that is?"

"Music?"

"Not just any music - Bach, Beethoven, Mozart. All right here in our living room," he said, smiling over at me.

"Who is Mozar?" asked Mitu.

My father smiled.

"Mozart. Not Mozar. He is our guest today. If you take all

the beauty in the world and make music from it – it will sound like this. An orchestra is playing this music, an orchestra of dozens of wonderful musicians who place their trust in one person who leads them to play everything perfectly. He's called a conductor!" My father began imitating the orchestra conductor with his arms. "Come join me, I'll teach you to lead the orchestra!"

When the music softened, his arms lowered, and in the moments that it grew in volume, he raised them high. When the tempo was fast, his hands moved quickly, and when it was slow, he accompanied it with smaller, by gentler move-ments. In the moments when he heard a single instrument, he pointed his arm at a certain part of the hall, and when the rest of the instruments joined in, he went back to conducting with both hands, and the children did the same, imitating his movements.

In the depths of the somber cave, in a godforsaken place, was a man, surrounded by a gang of street children, leading the Bucharest Philharmonic Orchestra. I could have sworn that even Matei, who stood to the side and smiled, was moved.

CHAPTER 9

Where is Catia?

Since the day he taught the children to conduct the orchestra , my father had assumed a more central role in the eyes of the children, and they became closer to us. I joined the rest of the children taking my turn on duty. It was risky, but we all had to do our part. We were four more people that had to be looked after. There were two additional reasons for going on the outside food excursions. One reason, my father knew about, the other. He did not. I asked to go with Nelu instead of Mitu.

We left at noon and slipped our way into the market. The supply was poor, but we still were able to gather some fruit and vegetables that had been thrown out as well as some we managed to grab without being caught. We went into some of the business places and asked if they had anything they could give us. People were not put off by this, apparently these days nomadic children were a common sight.

The moment I saw that we had enough food, I grabbed Nelu's arm and said, "Follow me."

Nelu didn't know where I was taking him, but as a good friend, he followed me. I led him to a street called Strada Bradului. He saw me standing stock-still in front of what had been Catia's house and was now a heap of rubble. Not only was Catia's house in ruins, the whole street looked as though life had been sucked out of it, as if a great storm had passed through and destroyed it and all its inhabitants. It was a central street in the Jewish neighborhood and I had no doubt about what had taken place there.

I made my way inside the rubble for a clue to her family's whereabouts. I rummaged through the objects scattered around the house like a madman, because I knew we could not stay there for long, but found nothing. We didn't know if anyone was watching us and getting suspicious, so we hurried back to The Fortress.

Two days later, I led Nelu to Griviţei Road to see what had become of our apartment. I promised my father I would be very careful. I knew how dangerous it was.

We got to Griviţei Road on the back roads. I didn't want to attract attention. Suddenly, I saw two policemen standing near my building. I didn't know why they were there, but I was not going to take a chance to find out, and I moved back quickly and hid behind the wall of the nearest street corner so they wouldn't see us. I realized it was time to get out of there.

"It's not safe here," said Nelu, "we should go back."

When Nelu spoke, I suddenly remembered what Catia told me that day in the park.

"Not yet. There is still one more place to go, and it's not close by."

I knew that Nelu wanted us to go back, but he understood that this was something important I had to do. He followed me reluctantly, and said nothing.

We reached the outskirts of Bucharest. Open fields and trees replaced the congestion of the buildings.

"Daniel, we have to get back to The Fortress before dark."

"Don't worry, Nelu, we'll be there in five minutes."

I stopped for a moment in front of the woods; there was something different about it. It was not the same; many trees were burned, and those still standing were bare - no leaves on the branches.

"What is it, why did we stop?"

"We're here," I said, pointing toward a nearby house.

The garden was unrecognizable. The ground was scorched, the beautiful plants and flowers gone, weeds growing in their place. The house looked deserted. I hurried inside. The door was off the hinges and I entered. Everything in the house was upside down, filthy. Traces of dried blood were on the carpet at the entrance, and shattered objects were all over the floor. I went through all the rooms, leaping over the debris. There was not a living soul. When I entered Catia's room on the second floor, I cracked. I fell to my knees with grief and buried my head in my hands. Suddenly I saw Catia's purse, the same purse that had brought me to The Fortress, sticking out from underneath the bed. I reached for it and the moment I held it in my hands I could not help myself and began to cry. For the first time I realized I would never see her again. If only I had come before... I thought, maybe I could have saved... Nelu came behind me and put his hand on my shoulder.

"I promised her mother I would protect her, and I did not keep my promise, how can I go on?"

Nelu's grip on my shoulders tightened.

Suddenly Nelu released his grip and went to the window - he seemed to notice something outside.

"Daniel, there's a man at the entrance to the house looking at us."

I got up, stared carefully through the window, and saw him. He looked straight at me, as if he knew we were inside.

We wanted to run out of the house, but he stood at the entranceway. We stopped in front of him.

"What are you looking for here, boys?" he asked.

"Excuse me sir," said Nelu, "we were just wandering around, we were about to go, we did not know we were interfering or doing anything wrong."

"You were. Don't hang around here, not near this house."

We should have turned and run, but I wanted some answers.

"Do you know what happened to the people who lived here?"

"What business is it of yours, boy?"

"Please, I have to know!" Something in my tone made him change his expression.

"All I can tell you is that the good people who lived here are no longer alive, dragged like animals out of the house in the middle of the night, and not far from here they were murdered by those bastards, those brutal animals.

"It can't be! It's not true!" I yelled as tears streamed from my eyes. "What do you even know?!"

"I'm sorry, boy, I'm telling the truth, did you know them?"

I could not bear to hear anymore. I started to run, and Nelu followed. We ran all the way back to the center of Bucharest until we reached the populated area, and only in one of the alleys did we stop for air. We continued on. I led, because I knew the area better than Nelu. We kept running. It seemed to me that I heard the sound of the gendarmerie[11] behind us, and indeed, when I looked back, I saw soldiers running after us! The closer we came to the Athenaeum, the more afraid we became that they would overtake us. We ran through the alleyways. At one point, Nelu raced past me. For a few minutes,

---

11   Gendarmerie – military units with power to enforce civil law

we still ran side by side, but the gap between us began to widen. I felt that at any moment, a hand might reach out and stop me, and I ran as hard as I could. I was exhausted, out of breath, but I knew that if I stopped, my life would be in danger. They shouted at us to halt, but we kept going. My strength was running out, and Nelu was already far ahead of me. As Nelu pulled away, I heard the soldiers behind me getting even closer. I didn't dare shout to Nelu. I didn't want him to turn around. I knew that if he saw me so far behind, he would stop, and I didn't want them to get both of us. The soldiers were only a few meters behind me and narrowing the gap. I couldn't keep running. I lost my balance and slammed down hard on the stone floor in the alley. My eyes closed for a moment, and in my imagination, I saw father, mother, Catia and Lili in front of me…" I'm sorry, Lili… I won't be able to tell you any more stories at night to put you to sleep. Sorry, Catia, for not being there to protect you. Sorry mom and dad, that I won't be able to look after Lili, Sorry I let you all down!"

A hand grabbed my shirt by the collar and held tightly. I knew I was finished; I didn't even try to struggle. I looked at the soldier who had caught me and he looked down at me. Why wasn't he shouting at me or hitting me? That's when I saw the surprised look in his eyes. It was my friend Ion. We stared at each other. There was no exchange of words like "My friend, how long since we saw each other!" And no: "Good to see you!" Merely one long, continuous stare. He was still holding onto the collar of my shirt and slowly let it fall from his hand.

He lowered his head and said something I could not understand.

After a few seconds, he raised his head and looked straight into my eyes.

"Run!"

For a moment, I was paralyzed, but I quickly realized I had to get away.

I nodded numbly at Ion and got to my feet. I saw Nelu from a distance running back toward me. I started to run without looking behind me.

I did not let Nelu stop when he got to me.

I grabbed his hand and shouted, "Run! This is no time to stop!"

We continued running like mad all the way to the Athenaeum. Only after we managed to get in through the window did we finally stop to catch our breath.

Nelu put his hand on my shoulder.

"I know how you feel, what it is to lose all hope, but you must not let it take you down, you have to keep faith, because if you don't, there will be nothing to keep you going."

"There's no point," I blurted out, and he shook me hard.

"Are you really so stupid that you can say something like that? What about your family, what about Lili, your mother, father? You think it's not hard for them? They need you, you can't let them down. Do you know what I would give for my sister and mother to be with me?"

And he took off his cap.

"Do you see this?"

"I promised that until I came back for my mother and sister, I wouldn't take it off, and I will go back for them, even if it's the last thing I ever do. Are you going to waste your time thinking about giving up when so many people are depending on you?"

I straightened up, took Nelu's cap from his hand and put it back on his head.

"You're right, Nelu."

CHAPTER 10

Ionel

I walked down the street carrying the mattress. It was not a big one, but bulky enough to make it hard for me to carry. I hauled it on my back and walked through the streets of Bucharest. I had only one direction I could think of. Piața Constituției (Constituției Square). The resolve I had been feeling when I left my father's apartment was replaced by apprehension, sadness, and regret. I realized I could not keep going on carrying the mattress, so I decided to hide it in one of the alleys. I dragged it to the middle of an alley where I saw cartons lying beside a large metal container. I propped the mattress up against the wall and covered it up with cartons so it couldn't be seen.

In all the places my father took me, in all the filthy apartments, there was only one thing that was always mine: my mattress. I shut my eyes and asked God, "Please, please, let the mattress still be here when I come back."

I left the alley and walked toward the square. When I reached the big square, I sat down on one of the benches and waited for the gang of street kids I used to hang out with to show up. The first time they saw me there I was sitting on the same bench. They had approached me and then asked if I wanted to hang out with them. I agreed because it was better than just sitting there on the bench, feeling how hungry I was. It was an hour or so when I saw three of them far off on the left side of the square. Two of them were following a boy named Corneliu. I got up and went toward them. I had often gone around with them for something to do until it got dark and I could go back to my father's apartment. The first time they saw me there I was sitting on the same bench. They had approached me and then asked if I wanted to hang out with them. I said yes like always. It was better than just sitting there on the bench, feeling how hungry I was.

I never had any friends. The only company I'd ever had was my mother, and since she died, we had moved around so much I never got to know other children. I did not go to school; I never invited anybody home to play. The only children I knew were the children from the square. They were the closest thing I had to friends. We usually walked the streets, and Corneliu and the two kids that followed him, Petru and Sandu, would harass people in the street, pushing, yelling, and at the first sign of trouble would run away. It was the only game I knew, besides roaming around the square begging for money from people passing by. With the spare coins we managed to beg, we would buy something to eat at the kiosk and divide it up. Many times that was the only food I put in my mouth all day long.

That day when I joined them I hoped I would get something to eat. At the end of the day, we managed to buy something to eat, and when it got dark, we all went back where we came from. I returned to the alley. I walked fearfully through the streets on the way, hoping the mattress would still be there. I kept telling myself that it would be. When I reached the alley, I saw the layer of cartons leaning up against the wall and for a moment, I felt calm, but as I got closer, I saw they seemed to be placed differently.

I feared the worst. I walked closer, grabbed the two larger cartons, and moved them aside. There was nothing behind them. I began to flip the cartons in all directions. The mattress was gone.

It was too much. I leaned up against the wall, my knees tucked up to my chest, my hands cupping them, my head curled down to my thighs, and I cried. I couldn't stop. I had no way of comforting myself. Suddenly all the sadness that had been building up in me since my mother's death burst out of me. I don't remember how long I was there, crying in that alley, under cover of darkness, but finally, I spread a few cartons on the ground and crawled between them. I wrapped myself in some empty bags, pulled the rest of the cartons on top of me, and fell asleep.

CHAPTER 11

Daniel

That conversation with Nelu changed something in me. I stopped feeling sorry for myself and started to concentrate on what I could do and not what I couldn't.

One day Lili was playing with some stones she had found. On a large piece of gray stone, she painted a swastika with a piece of coal and surrounded it with the juice of a rotten tomato - that stood for the enemy. On other white stones, she drew faces that represented us fighting the gray stone together.

"One day it will happen, right?" Lili asked me.

"What?"

"We'll beat them and be able to go outside! We'll play in the park and go to school… We'll be able to sit around the table and eat Mama's *clătite and sarmale*[12] and we'll laugh and talk… and we'll go back to the Athenaeum…"

"Of course it's going to happen, and besides, we're already at the Athenaeum!" I smiled at her. "If you stay as brave and strong as you are, in the end we'll win." I tried to convince her to believe in something I myself was not sure of.

---

12   *Clătite* - *Crepes* cooked fast in a hot pan and filled with some-thing sweet or savory, and *sarmale* – Romanian cabbage rolls.

I saw my father watching us from the corner and smiling. It had been a long time since I had seen him smile, and it made me happy. I told my parents about what I had seen near our apartment, but not about Catia's house. The memory of that scene was excruciating, and I did not want to inflict them with that pain.

Winter set in, full force. The weather conditions were harsh, food was scarce, and the blankets we had were not enough to protect us from the bitter cold at night.

The Athenaeum was the only thing that remained loyal to us and kept us in Bucharest. Even if some of its windows were smashed and some of its walls marred with swastikas - a reminder of that bloody day - in our eyes it still remained pure and majestic.

Rays of sunlight penetrated through the round opening covered with murky glass at the center of the dome, and illuminated the ground. Sometimes I would take Lili and we would stand in the light, close our eyes, feel the warmth on our faces and imagine ourselves walking on the banks of the Dâmbovița River on a sunny day. Those rays of light, which managed to reach us despite being unseen by every other human eye, reminded us that we had been born into a more beautiful world, and we were filled with hope that one day we would see it again.

The situation outside the Athenaeum was only getting worse. German soldiers began to circulate in the streets, and the heavy repression of the gendarmerie intensified even more.

Luckily, our daily "emissaries" did not attract too much attention in the streets, which were anyway filled with children dressed in rags, a sign of the terrible economic conditions the Nazis brought with them.

More than a year passed, and the fort became our home and our prison. The days were somber and we began to lose hope that life would get better. The only thing that occupied us was how to survive the day.

On birthdays, we would spread out one of the big blankets between us all and raise the celebrant in the middle. My mother would go up to the birthday boy and put a candy in his hand. To this day, I do not know how she got hold of those candies.

On Hanukkah, my father took out the menorah that had stood permanently on the windowsill of our apartment, and placed it at the entrance to the cave.

"I have no candles for it, but at least I was able to take it with me before we left the apartment, and like every year, we'll put it out for all to see." I was surprised when I saw the menorah. I was glad my father had managed to take it with him, because I knew what it meant to him. It had been in our family for generations. Yet it also made me sad to see it there, forlorn, without the light of the flickering Hanukkah candles.

When the other children asked about the menorah, my father told them what the Hanukkah menorah symbolized for the Jewish people. I saw Nicu gather the other children around him, and the next day we woke up with candles and some matches lying near the menorah. That evening we lit the candles and tried to teach the children the songs. On Crăciun (Christmas), we all joined in to build a tree like the fir tree and decorate it with scraps of branches we found in the streets, and the children taught us Christmas songs.

These little things, which in other circumstances might not have had such importance, gave us the will to go on, and above all, it showed us how united we had become.

One morning Doru came storming into our cave. I didn't

know the exact time, but the few rays of light filtering down indicated that we'd gotten through another cold, hard night.

"Constantin! Constantin!" Doru shouted hoarsely.

"You must come, come quickly."

"What is it, Doru?"

"Come quickly!"

My father got up right away and followed Doru. We all joined in behind.

"What's happened?"

"It's Dinu."

My father and Doru entered the cave where Dinu and Lizica slept. Dinu lay stretched out on the floor, covered with blankets, sweating and twitching.

My father stood at the mouth of the cave and moved the other children back.

"Let the child breathe, let him breathe." He went and sat down on the other side of Dinu and called Matei to come and help. "Daniel, bring some wash cloths and two more blankets here."

My mother came into the cave with some washcloths she had made from the remains of a torn blanket.

From that moment on, my father and mother did not move from Dinu's room. They put the damp washcloths on his forehead and changed them repeatedly. They took the two glass cups we had, heated them with matches and placed them face down on Dinu's bare back. They made sure he was covered, and spoke soothingly to him. Nevertheless, Dinu continued to worsen. It was hard for all of us to watch, helpless to do anything. Lizica took it the hardest. She stayed at the cave entrance, doing whatever my father asked, keeping her distance, but maintaining eye contact with Dinu. She stood there, the tears streaming down her cheeks while she waited for a sign from my father.

Dinu had a fever for two whole days. None of the children could sleep, but my mother and father asked us to leave them alone in the cave with Dinu, to leave room around him.

On the morning of the third day, my father came out of the cave for a moment. We saw him and went over towards him. It was raining that day, and drops trickled out of the cracks in the ceiling of the hall and made muddy puddles on the dusty ground.

The expression on my father's face was almost blank, but I could see the despair and the sorrow in his eyes.

He did not greet any of us; instead, he went over to stand beside Lizica.

He leaned down and looked into her weeping eyes.

"Why is God doing this?" she asked, trembling. "Is He punishing me because I have been such a bad girl? Because if He is, I promise... I promise... if only He will not hurt Dinu!" and she burst into tears again.

My father hugged her tightly.

"You are both wonderful children, and not only do we all love you, but God loves you too. Look how brave your brother is, and how he will not give up. If God didn't love him, do you think he would have made him so brave?"

Lizica stopped crying.

"Daniel, go and wet some more cloths."

"Do you know why it's raining, Lizica?"

"Why?"

"It rains because God and His angels see what bad things happen in this world and they begin to weep, and with their tears they wash away the evil."

"Isn't it true that after the rain, the air gets cooler and more pleasant, and there's a different smell all of a sudden?"

Lizica nodded in agreement.

"That's because the evil is washed away. You see the patches of wet cloth that Daniel has brought me, they are soaked in the tears of angels, the tears of God, and we use them to make Dinu better, but to make him strong, we have to be strong for him. Can you be strong for him, Lizica?"

She nodded, and he hugged her again. The rain fell all day, while waited for any change.

At night, I took my mother's place at Dinu's side so she could rest, and my father and I watched over the feverish Dinu until weariness overcame us both and we fell asleep.

In the middle of the night, we awoke to Lizica's footsteps. She moved from side to side in the cave and tugged at both our shoulders. She leaned in toward my father.

"Did you hear?" she whispered.

"Hear? No, I can't hear anything," my father replied, trying to awaken to recover from an all too short sleep.

"Shhh... Listen," she said.

"I don't hear anything, darling."

"The rain! The rain!"

"What about the rain? I don't hear anything."

"It's stopped!" She had a big grin on her face.

"If the rain stopped, that means... it means the evil has been washed away, isn't that right?"

My father immediately grasped her meaning. He leaned over toward Dinu and could not believe his eyes. There were no beads of perspiration on his face.

"Quickly, Daniel, give me the jug of water."

My father leaned over Dinu and gently lifted his head to his feet so he could drink.

Dinu's mouth opened slightly, and with his eyes closed, and his hand on the jug, he began slowly sipping the water.

"*Mori de foame*[13]," he muttered.

My father smiled.

"If he has an appetite, that's a good sign."

He felt Dinu's forehead.

"There's no more fever!"

"And that's good... right?" Lizica asked.

"Yes, dear... it's wonderful."

My father and mother continued to stay by Dinu and care for him. By evening Dinu began talking to them and to Lizica.

"I'm afraid," Dinu whispered in my mother's ear as he lay in her lap.

"Only the brave know fear, Dinu," she said, as she stroked his head and sang to him.

The morning came and brought with it good tidings - Dinu managed to get up on his feet.

Matei came in and said to him: "At last you're on your feet, but we're all falling off ours because of you, you little...!" And he stroked Dinu's hair in a rare display of affection.

It was hard to believe, but little Dinu recovered completely. From that moment on, my parents became everyone's parents, and all the children began to come to our cave to sit with them, listen to their tales of pre-war Bucharest and how we would all go to a restaurant to celebrate the end of the war one day. My father taught them history, music, he told them about the world, and they sat fascinated and listened to him. Even Matei began to visit, although standing outside, secretly, to listen to

---

13   *Mori de foame* – I'm starving.

the stories my mother and father would tell.

Dinu's recovery gave us all renewed strength to go on, but still, we lived in hiding. The persecutions outside continued and the streets of Bucharest were still dangerous for us. The end was nowhere in sight. We were one big family, and now more than ever, we supported and helped each other. "The Fortress Knights" we called ourselves; the only knights in the world who wore ragged clothes and had nothing to eat.

CHAPTER 12

Nelu

Two years, four months and two days passed in The Fortress. Two years, four months and two days of waiting. Many times, I was close to a breaking point, but I had a promise to keep.

There were nights in The Fortress when, all alone, I would imagine the day I would return. Every night I fell asleep with the same thoughts, the same pain. Time is passing, and I have not yet gone back for them.

One day I almost told Constantin. We were sitting and talking while Daniel and Lili stood in the center of the hall, enjoying the few rays of light that filtered in from the ceiling.

"How long have you been here, Nelu?"

"Almost two and a half years already."

"And you don't ever think about going home?"

"Every day, but my father is not like you, Mr. Lupescu, when I go back, it will be to get my mother and sister away from him. I want to be able to care for them. I want to be able to take care of the children here, too. This is no place for a child."

"I believe you, Nelu. A day will come when we will leave, and I will come visit you, your mother and your sister in your new home."

"I never told Daniel, but each day that went by I thought

about leaving, at least that's the way it was before the war started, now we have no choice but to stay here."

"Do you think our being here makes it harder for you?"

"Of course not, Constantin, the opposite. It's true that at first the children distrusted you, but now your being here steadies them and calms them."

"What do you mean?"

"Constantin, all the children here, and I am one of them, do not come from families that cared about them. We all came from families who threw us out on the street or beat us until we ran away."

Constantin turned his gaze to me.

"I'm beginning to understand why Daniel says you're a special person, Nelu, when I talk to you, sometimes I forget who's older, me or you," he said, smiling.

"Constantin, if something should ever happen to you..."

"What can happen? Everything will work out in the end. I hope you don't waste your time with frightening and unnecessary thoughts."

"Frightening, maybe, but not unnecessary. You should know that there are three caves on the third floor, full of holes. The other children don't go there because they are afraid of the dark tunnels, but it would be a great place to hide."

"And you? You're not afraid of them?"

I smiled.

"After more than two years here, I'm pretty sure there are no monsters in those caves."

It was remarkable how the Lupescu family joined with us in The Fortress. We came from such different worlds, and not only did Daniel and I become good friends, the whole Lupescu family, which at first seemed to the children as if they had come from another planet when they arrived, was eventually accepted and trusted.

At first, it was hard, because the children were not used to outsiders in The Fortress, but especially because of the contempt Matei had for them.

However, things began to change after Constantin found a way to reach the kids, and culminated when Clara and Constantin took care of Dinu and made him well.

CHAPTER 13

On Our Trail

One day we heard shouting in The Fortress. This was a rare event, since the children were quiet most of the time because Matei threatened them and told them never to shout.

It was Matei who was shouting. As we came out of the caves, we saw him clutching Mitu's torn and tattered shirt. Matei was almost lifting him up in the air.

"What's the matter?" I shouted.

He ignored me.

"How many times have I told you, and you took them straight to here! *Un prost facut gramada*[14]! What if they find us?!"

"What happened?"

"This idiot caught the attention of some of the idiot soldiers in gray uniforms on the street with the swastikas on the sleeve. They started chasing him. What did Mitu do? He couldn't lose them in the streets, so he decided to run straight here! It won't be long before they find us!"

Constantin moved nearer and placed his hand on Matei's arm.

"He only wanted to bring us food, what's done is done. Look

---

14   *Un prost facut gramada*! – You stupid fool!

what you are doing to his shirt; you're going to tear it to pieces."

Matei looked at Mitu and released his grip on the shirt. Mitu almost fell down.

"He's all yours, Constantin, maybe you'll be able to explain to this idiot what he did."

Mitu looked at me. "I didn't not mean to Nelu!" he cried bitterly. Constantin tried to calm him, but suddenly, a loud sound pierced the silence in The Fortress. We all looked up, startled, at the entrance to the cave. Within a few seconds, we heard voices. Not one person or two, but many, and shouts...

Constantin was the first to regain his senses.

"Quickly, everyone gather up all the things hanging outside and take them inside the caves with you, and stay there. Don't make any noise! Quickly, we don't have much time!"

The children stood looking at each other as if they didn't understand a word he was saying.

"Do you want to stay alive?!" Matei shouted. "Do as he says, now! Go!"

The children began running, grabbing their things and rushing into the caves.

I went to Constantin, who was helping the children together with Matei, all the while looking toward the entrance to The Fortress.

"For more than a year and a half, we have been living in this damned darkness, maybe now it will be to our benefit... You cannot harm what you can't see..."

"What do you mean, Constantin?"

"I was told once about a perfect place to hide..."

I immediately understood.

"Help me take lead everyone there, Nelu, we'll split up into two groups, each group into a separate cave."

We hurried to tell Daniel and Matei of the plan, and the four of us rushed everyone up and led them into the third-floor caves. We did not leave any tangible items to be seen, and we hoped that the paintings on the walls would be shrouded in the darkness.

Matei took Mitu, Rita, Nicu and Doru. Constantin and I entered the other with Daniel, Lili, Clara, Lizica and Dinu.

"Stay deep inside the cave and don't peek out, keep absolute silence, for hours if necessary, but do not dare leave the cave!"

Everyone entered except Daniel and me. We stayed outside, looking anxiously at each other.

Now, beams of light were seen coming from the entrance tunnel.

Constantin called us to come inside, and Daniel took my arm and pulled me into the cave.

We hid and listened. For a moment, there was silence that made us think that perhaps the threat had passed, but after a few seconds, the noises grew louder.

They came from the entrance tunnel.

"They're coming!" There were whispers inside the caves.

"Shh!"

We all sat in complete silence, but there was a storm raging within us. I had never been so scared. Constantin took Daniel's arm.

"They're here."

"Promise me, Daniel, that you'll look after Lili and Mama."

"Dad, this is not the time to..."

"Promise me, Daniel!"

He nodded.

"I am proud of you," he said, standing with his back to the opening of the cave, facing us.

***

"Sir, he came in here! I saw him run in here!"

"Find him for me, find the little Gypsy, and we'll take care of him."

"*Capul plecat sabia nu taie,*" whispered Constantin.

From time to time, a beam of light would flash and pass along the edge of the mouth of the cave. We could only pray that one of them would not illuminate inside the caves. Fear flared up in my body like fire. I heard every little noise, every clink of a shoe on The Fortress floor. I knew they would keep looking until they found us.

Suddenly, it happened. A single beam of light entered the cave, rose up quickly, and then, just before it went away, it stopped and reversed back toward the cave.

"Sir, there's a cave here!"

We kept silent. The light that had penetrated the cave grew stronger.

We heard footsteps. Each step louder and closer than the one before, each step nearer than the last.

Suddenly the footsteps stopped, and several beams of light penetrated deeper and deeper into the cave.

Constantin turned and walked toward the mouth of the cave.

"What is he doing? Don't take another step!" I wanted to hold him back, but I was too far away from him.

Daniel tried to grab his arm, without success. We wanted to shout out, but we knew that this way they would find us all, so we remained silent, helpless. Constantin was out of our reach and he stood there at the entrance to the cave, the beam of light shining at his feet.

A voice shattered the silence.

"Stupid Nazis! Looking for me? Here I am, I bet you can't catch me!"

There was no doubt, it was Matei's voice..

The beam suddenly changed direction and went down to the left, and then disappeared. We heard the sound of the footsteps moving away.

"Get him!"

"Filthy Nazis, even your fastest runner won't catch me alive!" Matei's mocking laugh was heard echoing in The Fortress.

"Get him and bring him to me now!" shrieked the officer.

We heard retreating footsteps heading back toward the tunnel.

"After him!"

There was a sudden rush of heavy footsteps, followed by a burst of gunfire echoing through the hall…then utter silence.

The footsteps stopped.

"We got him."

"Excellent, do a search around him and let's get out of this stinking hole."

"Take the Gypsy's body out with you, and everyone will see what happens when you deal with us."

The sound of footsteps moved off, along with the sound of something being dragged on the ground. Every fiber in my body wanted to rush toward them, but I knew I would endanger everyone.

It was too much. Finally, I gave in to my instincts and started to lean toward the mouth of the cave, ready to run out. Daniel grabbed my arm with a grip so strong that it paralyzed my arm at first, and slowly my whole body as well.

"Don't move!" he whispered to me with a stern look, although both of us wanted to run out of the cave after them.

The noises diminished until they finally stopped. Still, no one dared move.

The moments seemed like an eternity, until Daniel let go of my arm. Together we cautiously went out of the cave toward The Fortress hall, slowly followed by the others Nicu was already standing there with Constantin. They stopped in front of us in the middle of the hall and looked toward me and at Daniel. We saw the puddle of blood leading to the tunnel and we knew what to do without them having to ask. We gestured to the other children to stay back. Constantin entered the tunnel.

At first, I thought he wanted to make sure the soldiers were gone, but he stopped in front of the tunnel, knelt and examined the entrance. He picked something up from the tunnel floor. His body blocked his hands so I couldn't see what it was. He got up again and walked back toward us. Then stopped and regarded us somberly with his eyes.

"Get everyone back into the caves," he said, his expression blank.

"Dad, I think that—"

"Daniel, I said to get everyone back to the caves, no arguments, no noise, I am not sure we are safe yet."

We went back into the caves. We knew we had to be completely quiet, as did all the children - they were paralyzed with fear.

Constantin sat at the mouth of the cave and stared into the void all that night. He did not speak to any of us.

The harrowing night took its toll; no one could really sleep, or talk. In the middle of the night, I saw Constantin sitting in the doorway of the tunnel and keeping watch, exactly as he had been when we went into the caves. I approached him quietly.

"Constantin," I whispered.

He opened his fist and I saw in his hand what he had picked up in the tunnel. Pebbles, small stones, stained with blood... It was not into the void Constantin had been staring for hours, he was looking at those stones. Daniel woke up and joined us. Together we looked at the stones in Constantin's hands.

"This is all we have left of Matei," he said. "You need to be strong for the rest of the children. This is not the time to fall apart. Go to sleep, and if tomorrow is quiet, we will leave the cave and decide what to do."

Slowly I turned back to the caves. I didn't care if I had a cover, or a blanket under me or not. I just closed my eyes and instantly fell asleep.

I awoke to the touch of Constantin's hand on my shoulder.

"Wake the rest of the children and come and help me and Daniel, in Matei's cave."

We did what he said and together went into Matei's cave.

Constantin picked up Matei's staff that lay in the corner of the cave and went out, with me following him.

We still did not understand what he wanted to do. He turned to Daniel.

"I want you to have the children go through all the crevices and holes to gather as many stones as they can," he said, "as many as they possibly can."

We started to work. The children did not understand why they had to collect stones, and couldn't I explain it to them, because I myself was not sure I understood. In any case, for the next few hours that was all that occupied us. We knew it was for Matei, and everyone went about the task without complaint. Constantin called Daniel and me over to him and asked us to wipe out the path of blood that led to the tunnel so that the other children would not see it.

The children went through the caves and searched for stones in all of them. We all did it with heavy hearts. The feelings were deep. Constantin walked toward the cave on the first floor and asked the children not to enter it, but to lay the stones at the opening.

By noon, we were exhausted, and since Constantin knew that there was so little water and food, he called everyone to gather near the cave and asked us to go in.

Inside the cave, Constantin had created a circle of stones that surrounded Matei's staff along with the bloody pebbles. The staff and pebbles were laid in the ground in the center of the cave.

"First, I want to thank you all for your effort. You did it for your friend, and I want us all to gather around the circle."

I began to understand what Constantin wanted. I took off my cap and stood by the circle of stones, my head bowed low.

"From now on, this will be Matei's room," Daniel's father began. "We have set up a monument here for a man who, yesterday, did the noblest act a man can do... He sacrificed his life so that others could live, and saved us all. We should all remember every time we enter this room, that we must survive and get through this, to show him that his sacrifice for us was not in vain. Agreed?"

"Yes," a faint murmur came from Lizica and Dinu.

"We will not leave here until I hear all of you say that, so I ask again, do you agree?"

"Yes," everyone replied.

"Do you think Matei deserves it?!"

"Yes!" This time everyone's voices echoed loudly throughout the fort.

Constantin closed his eyes and bowed his head, as did the children after him.

There was silence. It was hard to believe how that gang of urchins I met when I first came to the fort had become so noble in those moments. It was out of respect for Matei... the boy with the staff who had cared for no one and for whom no one had cared... That tough boy who never smiled and made us think he had a heart of stone. It turned out he had the biggest heart of all. How we missed him now...

CHAPTER 14

Daniel

Our thoughts were mostly focused on Matei that same day, but everyone feared the soldiers might return, and we were no longer safe in the fortress.

"I don't know what's waiting for us out there, but I do know what's waiting for us in here. We can't stay here much longer," my father said.

He made sure to sit with all the children and talk to them about what happened to Matei and how we have to move on from here. He knew it was a matter of time before the soldiers came back. Some of them were sure to notice that the boy they had killed was not Mitu, and that he was not alone. We had lived in The Fortress almost a year and a half, and through all that had happened we have always felt protected there. This was suddenly changed now. It was hard for me to face the fact that we would soon have to leave it, because that was not how we wanted to go free of it. We had hoped to walk out with heads held high, not bowed, hopefully, not fearfully. Now the crucial question arose: If we must leave The Fortress, where would we go?

I suggested to my father that I would check on our apartment again when I went on one of our food excursions, and he agreed.

I went out with Nelu at dusk so as not to attract attention, especially in an area that was so dangerous.

We reached Griviței Road. I was afraid they would find us again, but this time there were no uniformed men in the area. We approached the apartment from the other side of the street, slowly and carefully.

The apartment looked the same from outside. I was so happy to see it. The house had not been damaged. It was beautiful as always and now we could all go back! I began to cross the street, but as I approached, I could see a light coming from the living room window that faced the street. I walked past the building and peered through the window in silence. A boy was seated at the table and to his right was a woman who served him a plate with *Mămăligă*[15] and *Tocanita cu galuste*[16]. I had not eaten such dishes for a long, long time. An elderly man sat next to the boy, eating *Mancare de cartofi*[17]. The woman sat down next to them, and for a moment, I felt a terrible longing. It reminded me of the normal life

I had a year and a half ago, and I wanted it back, but now another family was sitting in my house eating from my table, on dishes that I used to eat from...

I wanted to yell, so they would know this was impossible to accept!

I curled my hand into a tight fist and hammered on the window furiously, then ran away quickly, not only so as not

---

15   Mămăligă is a porridge made out of yellow maize flour, a tradition in Romania

16   Tocanita cu galuste is meat with dumplings

17   Mancare de cartofi – a dish made with potatoes

to get into trouble, but also because I couldn't stand to look anymore; what I saw hurt too much. My house had been stolen from me, and I would never be able to return to it.

I ran and ran, not knowing where. I ran as hard and far as I could with Nelu following me. We finally got back to the fortress and I told my father what I had seen. As I described to him, I suddenly remembered what Nelu had said - we have to concentrate on what can be done, and I had an idea. We had somewhere else to go, a place we would not be noticed and could hide. Catia's house on the outskirts of Bucharest! I shared my idea with my father, and together we began to plan the departure from The Fortress. We would have to check if the house was still abandoned, and if it was, we would have to walk there on the side roads in the middle of the night so we wouldn't be seen.

If we were lucky enough to reach it, we could find shelter there for a few months and then decide what to do.

The next day I was sent to the abandoned house together with Nelu. I had no doubt that I could remember how to get there. I made sure to check every building and every turn. I measured my steps. I checked that each passageway could hold all of us without attracting attention. I felt more than ever a heavy responsibility resting on my shoulders.

We arrived at the house. It was as deserted as before. Nelu and I stayed for a while to make sure no one was hanging around the place, for whatever reason. When we got back to the fortress and told my father, the decision was taken.

It was time to leave. We would go in the early hours of the morning, under cover of darkness, and hike all together to the house.

Before noon, we would be outside the city limits of Bucharest, and with a bit of luck we would not be noticed. We would use the light of dawn to show us the way to the house.

My father and I told everyone the plan. We knew that for the children to leave The Fortress without regret, they would have to believe they were going to a better place, So I described the house to them, with the garden, the trees and the grass, and all of us dared to dream of freedom. We explained to them that they had to sleep well that night, because we had a long march ahead of us. At last, we would have a real home to sleep in.

Nelu and I carefully went over all the roads we had taken. We wanted to be certain that we were in complete agreement on the way there, so that we could meet only at the house on the outskirts of Bucharest. It was important not to run into each other's group and draw attention to ourselves.

The children gathered their best blankets, worn and torn as they were, and the few things they had left, and went to sleep in the fortress for the last time.

"Daniel," Lili turned to me, "I'm afraid ... what if ..."

"Don't worry, Lili, just imagine what it will be like, playing in the garden, running around on the grass, closing our eyes and feeling the sun's rays caressing us, and sensing the wind carrying with it the scent of fields and flowers. I lay down next to my little sister and stroked her hair until she fell asleep. I did not close my eyes all night, because each time I did, I felt the burden of responsibility on my shoulders.

My father and I woke all the others an hour before sunrise. We ate leftover bread and began to exit the fortress. We decided to go out in two groups so as not to attract attention. One group with me, the other with Nelu. We were the only ones who knew the way.

We moved toward the entrance tunnel and went through it one by one. I waited for everyone to enter the tunnel, and then I went. I took one last look at 'the house' that I would never live in again. It was my prison, but it kept me safe. I got used to it and became dependent on it, and now it was if it were imploring me to stay, telling me not to abandon it, but we both knew we would not see each other again. I bowed to The Fortress and thanked it for everything. I knew now why fate had brought us together, and why today, we had to separate.

We left the tunnel, entered the dark space, and crawled until we reached the bathroom. We filled the bottles we had taken with us with water. We climbed the stairs, went quietly out of the window, one by one, and started walking.

Nelu was first, followed by Nicu, Doru, Rita and Mitu. A few minutes later my father, my mother, Lili, Lizica, Dinu and I, followed. This time I did not have the courage to look back. I had said goodbye to so many things in so short a time... I had to concentrate on the present and lead everyone to the new house as quickly as I could.

Now we walked along quietly through the narrow side streets, with their smooth, protruding stones, and along the drainage ditches. Above us, we saw rows of stretched clothes-lines with clothing hanging in the cold wind the night had brought with it. We stopped occasionally to snatch some clothes. This was our only chance to have something decent to wear, and an opportunity to cover our ragged clothes. We moved quickly and quietly all along the way.

Slowly the sun caught up with us. It was past the dawn, and daylight was shining over Bucharest. Every little noise startled us. We stopped to make sure no soldiers were about, and went on.

We made our way through the side streets, one by one, and in the instances when we heard the marching of soldiers, we slipped into one of the side streets and hid, as we had agreed upon in advance.

Every time we heard a shout. It frightened us. We were afraid it had to do with the other group of children. We all hoped everyone was making progress towards our destination.

The road seemed longer than I remembered, and the sun was rising. People began to appear on the street, which raised our level of tension, but we had already crossed the more dense area of central Bucharest, and had reached the less congested part. Slowly we began to see the environs around Bucharest that the buildings had covered.

We continued walking quickly, knowing it was impossible to stop. We finally reached the dirt road where we were heading. Only then, as green fields stretched out in front of us, and after we had left the main street, did a feeling of freedom begin to enter my consciousness for the first time.

We made no stops. It was important to keep moving. Something about this sunny day and the planted fields lent us a sense of relief. We passed some farmers eating bread with *slănină*[18]* and my father greeted them.

Lizica and Dinu began to tire, but we could not stop, not when we were so close.

Lizica began dragging her feet. She was so small and gaunt. My father picked her up and took her on his back. She hugged him around his neck, and he carried her along.

After about three miles on the dirt road, it split into two

---

18   Slănină - bacon, mainly made with fat from the back of the pig. Traditional Eastern European food.

paths, the one on the right led to the house. We stood on the hill and looked ahead of us. The path sloped through the trees, which hid the house. Nelu and his group were not on the horizon…had anything happened to them? Or had they already made it?

"The house is behind those trees," I said, pointing in the direction of the trees.

We continued on our way over the hill, and trees, and there was the house!

It was by all appearances deserted, the nearby earth scorched, the house surrounded by a neglected field of weeds and thorns. I told everyone to wait by the trees. I moved cautiously alone to see if someone might be in the house, and only after I had made sure that there was no sign of anyone, did I motion my group to approach.

It looked like someone had put the uprooted door back on its hinges. I heard voices on the other side of the door and footsteps coming closer. Did someone take over the house? Did I not notice and risk the lives of everyone when I signaled them to come closer? Did we come all this way for nothing? Maybe we should run away?

Before I could think of any more scenarios, the door opened wide with a creak...

It was Nelu.

"Welcome brother, you are invited to enter my house," he smiled.

I grabbed him and hugged him.

"Nelu, is everyone okay? are they all with you?"

"What do you think? After all we've gone through, 20 more miles is going to stop us?" He said, and a big grin spread across his face. We all entered the house and hugged each other, happy to see everyone safe and sound.

"And the house? Is there anyone inside? I mean, except for you? Maybe ..."

He put his hand on my shoulder.

"We checked... it's empty ..."

Lizica got down off my father's back, hugged everyone, and started running around the house.

"Is this our new house?"

"Yes, Lizica."

She cried excitedly to Dinu. "Look! Look what a beautiful house!"

There was something special about Lizica's childish innocence. It warmed my heart. Although she had been through so many terrible things that a girl her age should not have to experience, or perhaps because of it, she was still grateful for everything.

The thought that we would have a home to live in, and that the other children would have a normal structured routine, made me very happy.

Still, I had mixed feelings. I went upstairs to Catia's room, and when I went in, I saw her purse lying on the dresser. It had been there since Nelu and I were here the last time. The room was as messy as the rest of the house. The walls were dirty, objects were lying scattered everywhere, but the purse and the bed seemed to be intact. I sat down on the bed and held the purse in my lap. I wanted to feel her close to me, to ask her forgiveness for not being there for her. I was in the house we agreed to meet should something happen, but without her.

I lay down in her bed. I felt the soft welcoming mattress, the sheet enfolding me gently, inviting me to fall asleep. Suddenly I felt a pleasant chill, as soft as Catia's touch. I closed my eyes and saw her in front of me, smiling in the sunshine. Her smooth hair radiant in the light, her big brown eyes gazing at me, lifting all my worries from my heart. I knew that Catia had disappeared from my life and that I would not see her again, but that day I fell asleep with the sensation that she was with me.

I slept as I had not been able to sleep such a long time. All my dreams began and ended with her beaming face. In the morning, I awoke for the first time in a while without feeling apprehensive, but the pain from Catia's absence struck me when I realized that it was all but a dream.

CHAPTER 15

The New House

It was the winter of 1942 when we got to the new house. The days following our journey were accompanied by a great sense of relief. Not only did we get to the house just before the harsh days of winter, but also the adjustment to the new house, leaving behind the memories of The Fortress, was quick and pleasant.

The place had been neglected, but still, it was a house, and everyone was prepared to help repair it. For the first few days, the temperature outside was below zero and it was snowing. My father would not allow the children to go out into the garden and made sure they didn't holler and make too much noise playing to avoid drawing any unnecessary attention to the house from outside. With time, however, the fear lessened, because the house was isolated and well hidden from the main road, so none of us encountered people walking around the area. Far off on the horizon we could see another house. I remembered that Catia had told me about her parents' friends, but we did not want to attract being noticed, so I did not dare go near it.

Each time we went outside and felt the falling snowflakes, caught a few rays of the hidden sun, and breathed fresh air, instead of the damp and moldiness of The Fortress, it gave us a sense of freedom. There was no need for anything more, and there was nothing more.

My father wasted no time. The day after we arrived, he set off early in the morning for Bucharest and came back only at night. When he arrived, he shuffled into the kitchen with his last ounce of strength. We watched him anxiously as he spilled out food from the bag he had taken with him in the morning. Every day, weather permitting, he would do the same: leave at sunrise and come back in the darkness, and with his remaining strength, empty out the contents of the sack onto the kitchen table.

At first, he brought flour, sugar and beans. On the third night, he brought just vegetables - mainly potatoes, celery, carrots, cabbage and corn. The vegetables and everything else we could store, we took down to the cellar. We knew that when the snowy season came, there would be less possibility to obtain food.

Despite my asking him many times, my father would not let anyone else go with him. He knew that every day he went back to the center of Bucharest, he took a great risk, and he didn't want to put anyone else in danger. He never told us how he managed to gather the food, but it was clear to all of us how much effort it took. I would wait at night until he came back, and I could see him from the window, dragging himself to the doorway. I never went downstairs to the living room. I knew he would not want me to see him like that, lying on the couch, completely worn out.

In March, as the snow and ice began to thaw, we cultivated the garden, planted what we could - potatoes and tomatoes were first. Later we planted beans, corn, carrots and all the other seeds my father could bring back from the market. We planted as much as we could. About 100 meters from the grove was a well that was shared by the few houses in the area. We found four buckets outside the house, and went to the well to fill them, two or three of us at a time. We went very early in the morning, so as not to be noticed. Sometimes, the amount of water we brought back was not enough, and we would have to go back to the well again during the day. Nevertheless, we could not ask for more than that; compared to The Fortress, the world in which we now lived was infinitely more abundant. My mother would cook on a Primus stove we found inside the house and, if there were enough kindling, she would cook us a meal in the big wood stove. We usually preferred not to use it, because the smoke was a sure sign that there were people living in the house. From time to time, my mother made homemade *Papanași*[19] from eggs, semolina, cheese, and sugar. She put them in the boiling water one lump at a time, and then, while they were still warm, she would take them out and roll them in breadcrumbs and sugar. This homemade *Papanași* always reminded me of the Sunday meals in our apartment on Griviței Road. It seemed so far away. Each time mother prepared *Mămăligă*[20], she would put some of it to dry and then break it into pieces, so we would have something to eat when food was scarce.

We took care of the back garden only, leaving the grass in the front untended. My father made Lili, Lizica, and Dinu responsible for the work, and showed them how to plant everything. I still remember how every morning they would

---

19   *Papanași*– Fried cheese donuts, a popular Romanian dessert.

20   *Mamaliga* – Porridge made from yellow maize flour

run out to the garden to see if any seeds had sprouted. They would stare at the ground all day, fascinated, waiting for the plants to grow in front of their eyes. The spring days were sunny, with clear blue skies. The garden thrived and Romania's countless shades of green returned to the trees and nearby hills. It was wonderful to see. Summer days were hot, and the only blessed relief was from occasional rain that helped cool the stone path leading to the house. Sometimes the stones got so hot we could see steam rising from them as they dried off from the showers. These were happy days, full of a joy we had forgotten existed.

One morning, as was my habit, I awoke early and so did Nelu. We went to draw water from the well. We picked up the four empty buckets and started out. About fifty meters into the woods, Nelu stopped and grabbed my arm.

"Did you hear that?"

"What?"

"Never mind, come on, quick."

We picked up the pace and continued walking. A few meters before we reached the well, Nelu again stopped.

"What's happening with you today, Nelu? We have to hurry, come on!"

"Daniel," he whispered, pointing towards the woods.

"We are not alone."

I looked around, but saw no one. We got to the well and filled the buckets quickly so we could get away from there fast. We started back.

Just for a moment, I thought I felt someone passing behind me. I turned, but there was no one there. When I turned around to the well, I saw a figure in a brown robe with a large hood over its head. A bad omen. The figure looked up in our direction, and we did not know how to react. We didn't want to let on we were coming from the direction of the house. The figure moved quickly. This was someone sent to spy on us, I thought. At that very moment, Nelu and I knew we would have to confront the man in the hood, and when he realized that we were after him, he ran. We raced through the woods. We had to catch him; it could be a matter of life and death. We ran on either side of him, but Nelu was faster than I was, and narrowed the gap between us and the fleeing figure. Just at the edge of the woods, he tackled the hooded figure and wrestled it to the ground. A bastard spy! We would take him to the house and interrogate him. He was lying on the ground. Nelu grabbed the arms of the reclining figure, and I pulled off his hood, ready to strike him. Nothing could have prepared me for what I saw… this was no spy, it was… Catia!

"Catia! Is it you?!"

Her hair was disheveled, her expression somber, and she was thinner than I remembered, but I would know that face anywhere, anytime.

She looked at me excitedly and reached her hand out for my face.

Then she smiled her special smile and nodded, "Daniel!"

We picked her up off the ground gently and we both hugged for a long time. It was hard for me to let go of her. I thought that if I did, I might wake up and find it was all a dream.

Catia took my face in her hands, and kissed me. This time it was not a dream.

"We have to be quiet, come with me, quickly."

Catia led us to a house on the other side of the wood. Despite my father's warnings not to stray, we followed her.

Many questions ran through my mind, but we had to be

quiet, so we followed her without a word. The house she led us to was white, and larger than ours. It was surrounded by flowers and a green driveway lined with pebbles led to a staircase. Catia took us into the house. To the right of the entrance stood a wide table, and Catia motioned us to sit down next to it.

"They haven't come back yet, so we're alone. Would you like something to drink?"

"Who? Who isn't back yet? And what are you doing here?"

I could only stare at Catia and still wonder if I was dreaming. After all, we had gone through, I could not believe I was sitting with her, looking right at her.

"I saw all of you outside the house when the spring came. I couldn't believe it, but it was too dangerous to approach. Every week for the past two years, I have gone to the house to straighten things up a bit, being careful not to attract attention. They warned me not to, but I couldn't help it. I stopped going there only when the snow started this year."

Catia told us how her parents decided to pack what they could and flee to the house on the outskirts of Bucharest when the riots began in the neighborhood. At first, it seemed a wise move, but before long, word spread that the angry mob would reach us, since it was known that many Jewish families lived here.

Next door to her parents' house lived Maria and Gabriel, their friends, with their daughter Zsuzsika. One night, Gabriel and Maria came to the house where Catia and her parents lived to warn them. They had seen a group of villagers advancing with torches, and it was clear they were looking for Jews.

Soon, cries and shouts were heard in the distance. Catia's parents hoped that the villagers would pass by the houses and not come near, but to be on the safe side they sent Catia to

Maria and Gabriel's house to hide in Zsuzsika's room on the second floor at the back of the house, so she would not be seen by anyone passing in front. Maria and Gabriel locked the door of the room where the girls were hiding, and closed the windows for safety.

They waited in silence, but after a time, Catia began to hear shouts, and it seemed to her that the area near the back of the house was illuminated. Something was very wrong. She tried to open the door of the room, she begged Zsuzsika to open it, but it was locked. The girls banged on the door, but there was no response. Catia sprang to a window and with great effort managed to pull it open. "Stay in here and don't make any noise!" she said to Zsuzsika.

Catia slid down the tile roof, but lost her balance and fell. She managed to catch herself on one of the gutters, which broke her fall and probably saved her life. She landed hard on the ground and sprained her left ankle but immediately got up to see the sparks flying in the air, and suddenly understood the lights she had seen in the darkness came from her house. Some trees and a section of the garden of her parents' house were in flames. The fire threatened to engulf the house. All around were glass fragments and scattered pieces of furniture. Catia wanted to run over to the house, but she suddenly felt Gabriel behind her, holding her back. He held on to her until the mob moved on. "You can't go there, there's no point." He broke down in tears as he was holding her, but he could not let go of her until the mob moved on. He had promised her parents.

Although Gabriel tried to keep her from running to the house, she finally shook off his grip, and ran with all her strength towards the house, shouting to her parents.

Maria and Zsuzsika followed her, and together with Gabriel,

they started to put out the fire. Catia wept bitter tears. They managed to extinguish the flames, but they could not find Catia's parents although they searched into the night. Gabriel had three of his workers join them. One went with Catia and Maria, the other went out alone and the third joined with Gabriel and Zsuzsika.

Catia cried out her parents' names so many times she thought she would lose her voice for good. She was furious with herself for not staying with them, and would not stop until her screams were reduced to hoarse whispers. Still there was no sign of them. Gabriel tried to console her by saying they could be hiding, waiting for things to settle down to return, as that was what they told him they might do.

Two days she waited for them to come back, but no one appeared. Finally, she went to central Bucharest to see her old house in case they were there. There wasn't a living soul there. If her parents had been at the home, they would have left a sign for her. She searched the house, turning everything over and finding no sign of them. But her white purse, which she took with her. She went to Griviței Road and saw what happened to our apartment. Devastated, she returned to Maria and Gabriel, but she didn't give up. Ever since that day, she would go to the woods and stare at the house, waiting in vain for her parents and us to return. She knew she couldn't stay in the house. It was to dangerous, but she had to leave a sign, a sign seen only for those who knew her. She took her grandmother's handkerchief out of her purse and left the purse on the dresser. She kept the bad intact. Waiting. Once a week she would go to their home in the center of Bucharest to see if there was any sign. From them, or from us.

Maria and Gabriel had taken Catia into their home after

the night of the fire. Still, Catia did not give up, and went to the old house often. However, when the situation grew more dangerous in the streets, she accepted Maria and Gabriel's appeal to minimize her searches in the city center.

One day when she was watching the house, she saw someone outside. She thought the figure she saw was Nelu but she wasn't sure, so she ran to tell Gabriel. Gabriel told her it was too dangerous to go near the house, so she avoided doing so. Today she saw Nelu and me as we approached the well, and decided to follow us. She could not believe it was we, so she covered herself and watched quietly.

Catia called Zsuzsika to come meet us, and soon after that, Gabriel and Maria returned from work in the cornfields and entered the house. When Gabriel came in, Nelu and I fell silent. He was the old man who had driven us away from the house the first time we had been there.

"This is dear Gabriel and his wife Maria," said Catia.

"Hello," said Maria, "I've heard so much about you I feel we already know. I was wondering how long Catia could hold back before she invited you to our house."

"We met Gabriel already," snapped Nelu.

Gabriel came over to him and put his hand on his shoulder. Nelu flinched back a little.

"I was looking out for Catia. I did not know who you were that day, so I ran you off. I thought you were from a gang of drifters looking for a place to squat in. I've chased so many of them off, I got used to being aggressive, threatening them with my gun before they had a chance to see anything. I am sorry boys, but I'm glad you're here now."

"We are too."

We had to get back to our house so my mother would not

worry. Catia joined us to surprise her. And what a surprise it was... My mother almost dropped the boiling pot when she saw her. She threw herself at Catia and hugged her tightly, as did everyone else in the house. Catia sat with us and listened to all our stories from the time we arrived at The Fortress. Our experiences in The Fortress suddenly seemed so distant, but then she asked about Matei. We all felt the open wound in our hearts. It was too hard to talk about. In the short time remaining before dark, I told her about my family's escape from the Bucharest apartment to The Fortress, about my search for her, and about life in The Fortress, the brush with the soldiers, and all the rest that I could remember. She in turn told us about what had happened to her and life in the village.

It was dark by then, but we did not want Catia to go without seeing my father, so we all went back to Catia's house to introduce ourselves and ask Maria and Gabriel for permission for Catia to stay for a while. I promised them I would bring her back.

When my father finally came back home and saw Catia, he was stunned. When he hugged her, it was the only time in my life that I saw him shed a tear.

I told Catia that I had lost all hope of finding her, but that I had dreamed about her almost every night, and for her part, she told me how her faith that we would see each other again had weakened after her parents disappeared.

Catia was with me again. No longer a dream, not a hallucination. She was right before my eyes. I could touch her again, hug her, and kiss her. That day I knew that one must never stop believing. I promised myself I would not lose her ever again, even if I had to pay for it with my life.

CHAPTER 16

Ionel

Often, when I closed my eyes as I lay among the cartons at night, I imagined myself sleeping on the mattress in the apartment. I did not think it was possible, but I even missed my father. I didn't think that anything could be harder than it was with my father. I was angry with myself. I had made a mistake by leaving the apartment. Now as I lay in the freezing cold of the Bucharest night, the apartment was all I could think of. When my mother died, they told me God worked in mysterious ways. I tried to keep believing it. I tried, because that's what my mother used to say to me - you need patience to discover why things happen the way they do, even if at the moment we don't understand, in the end we will know why.

She had so much patience that she wanted to convey to me. Even at times when the illness seemed to wear her down, she always had a smile for me, always stroked my hand, even when my father used to shout at her.

In those bewildering days I spent alone in the alley, it was the memory of her patience that helped me most. I would repeat her words every time I thought I couldn't stand it anymore.

One day I was going around with Corneliu and the other children in the square. We started walking toward Bulevardul

Unirii, as we often did; running back and forth along the avenue, begging for handouts from passersby, and usually being
ignored. Nevertheless, every once in a while, just occasionally,
someone would give us a few pennies. For the most part, I
was shy, but I soon saw that this was the only way to survive,
so I did not stop myself from begging from the people on the
avenue and in the square.

That day was different. We started out, and about a hundred
yards down the avenue the others suddenly stopped. I thought
maybe Corneliu wanted to catch his breath, or go back to the
square, but he just stopped and stared straight ahead. I saw
two boys approaching us. Just as they did, Corneliu began
to run toward them. Corneliu. When the other boys passed
us, he suddenly swerved and bumped hard into one of them,
slamming him to the ground. Corneliu stood hovering over
the boy. It was clear he was not going to say "excuse me"
because I saw a threatening look in his eyes. He leaned down;
pulled the hat the boy was wearing off his head and put it on
his own. He did this without taking his eyes off the boy who
was lying sprawled on the ground.

The friend of the boy on the ground wanted to help him up,
but Petru and Sandu stood in front of him, blocking his way,
as if they knew in advance what to do while Corneliu grabbed
the boy's hat. Something else happened at that moment. I
understood something about Corneliu. He was dangerous. He
had no need of a hat. I don't think he even wanted it. What he
did to the other boy was only to terrorize him and show that
he was stronger and better. Corneliu continued walking, and
only then did Petru and Sandu let the other boy go over to
his friend and help him up. We all ran quickly to catch up to
Corneliu.

There was something about him, something everyone knew was there inside and should never be awakened. From that day on, I didn't think of the running around in the square as a game anymore. I did it because it was the only way I was able to put food in my mouth. Between my constant hunger and the pile of cartons at night, it was the only thing that kept me going. I knew it would not end well, but I could think of no other way forward. I had to do what I could do to survive.

This became my routine - the corner of the alley between the garbage can and the wall, a few cartons spread out, and the running around. Every day I woke up and went to the square to hang out with the others until dark. We usually begged in the square and on the boulevard, and the pennies people gave us were counted only in the afternoon so that we could buy something to eat at the kiosk. Sometimes someone would give us food, and sometimes we would go around the tables in one of the coffee shops, asking the diners for some of their food and picking up left overs, until one of the waiters would show up and scare us away. We ran around until dark, and then everyone went their own way. After what happened the day Corneliu attacked the boy, I started going back to my alley earlier. I did not tell anyone where I was going. I said my parents wanted me to come home early. I don't know whether it was from shame, or fear they would want to hang out with me at night, too.

Instead of my mattress, the only thing waiting for me those days was the pile of cartons and some bags. I started collecting newspapers to stuff them into my clothes before I went to bed. It helped warm me up. It was only the beginning of winter, and I knew as soon as it started to snow, nothing would help. Sometimes I would take the cartons and try to find an alleyway that would give me better shelter from the cold.

One night I put down the pile of cardboard boxes in a place I had been two days earlier. I thought about the days at the apartment, imagined my mother singing to me before bedtime and stroking my head, and again the tears started. I tried to stop them, tried to stay strong, but I couldn't. The tears rushed out uncontrollably, and I lay down on the cartons, stuffed newspapers into my clothes, covered myself with bags, put another pile of cartons on top of me, and continued to cry until I fell asleep.

The next night I woke up to strange noises on the street. Sometimes I would wake up from noises at night, but I had no one to turn to for help and I nervously waited for the clamor to stop. All I could do was curl up in the pile of cardboard boxes and hope it would go away, and that whoever was making it wouldn't notice me so I could fall asleep again.

However, that night the noise grew louder and louder, and as I tried to shrink into the cartons, I heard the sound of footsteps approaching. I tried to believe it was my imagination so I wouldn't panic. "A little more," I thought. "A little more and it will turn out to be just my imagination and disappear."

I waited for it to stop, and just as I started to believe that it was stopping, I heard a voice above the cartons.

"Hello…"

CHAPTER 17

Nelu

We stood, dressed in our rags, carrying our few possessions, and looked toward The Fortress, probably for the last time. I had been there two years, four months and fourteen days. Had it really been that long? How could I have let time pass that way when I had so many important things ahead of me? Something inside me was glad when we were leaving, because I had gotten used to The Fortress and that made me stray from my promise. When I thought of Catia's house, where we could live and go outside to enjoy the daylight whenever we wanted, it made me happy.

We left first: Nicu, Rita, Doru, Mitu, and me. The Lupescu family, together with Lizica and Dinu, followed behind us, and then we immediately split up.

I remembered the way. If there is one thing I have, it is a good memory, but it was still not easy to walk on in the cold, gloomy night in the streets of Bucharest. The road seemed longer somehow. As daylight drew closer, we were afraid that soldiers would see us and stop us for inspection. Soldiers could pop up anywhere because they often roamed the streets in those days. We passed the center of the city and reached the open areas. When the light of day lit up the green fields and hayfields ahead, I remembered sights I had seen as a child in the village. Those landscapes were one of the few good childhood memories I could recall. When we reached the woods, we saw the house from a distance. Nicu and Doru stopped to check with me that the house behind the wood was the one we were supposed to go to, and as soon as I nodded, they moved forward quickly, all excited. They deserved this excitement, and to be honest, I was enthusiastic as well. I had an odd feeling that someone was watching us, but I had a good look around, and there was no one else there. We entered the house one by one, with cries of joy. I hurried after them, and when I reached the doorway, something happened to me...

I thought of my house, where I had left my mother and my sister. For the first time in a long while, as I stood at the door of the house amid everybody's joy, I felt detached, that my journey was far from over. I did not feel truly free.

Everyone was cheering, and no one noticed a figure approaching the house. I peered through the curtain. Daniel! I went to the door and quickly opened it.

"Welcome, big brother, welcome to my house." He came over and hugged me.

Daniel checked that we had all arrived safely.

As I had expected, Lizica and Dinu were the most thrilled. They started running and jumping all around the house. Although things were scattered everywhere, the walls were charred at the entrance, and weeds grew in the garden and on the sides of the house, the atmosphere was warm and cozy. I found it hard to understand why. Maybe because I knew who had lived there before, maybe because of the surrounding landscape, maybe because we all just wanted to feel at home. A house is where you rest your body. A home is where you rest your soul .

On the lower floor was the large living room, kitchen, study and bathroom. The upper floor had three more rooms and an attic above. There were only two beds upstairs, one small one and a larger one. In the attic, we found a few mattresses and spread them in all the rooms. The big bedroom was for Constantin, Clara, Lili, Lizica, and Dinu. Nicu, Mitu, Doru and Rita took Catia's room, and Daniel and I took the third small room. Ours was the only one without a bed. We slept on the mattresses only. In the rest of the rooms, they took turns sleeping on a mattress on the floor and in the beds. Compared to the conditions we had in The Fortress for the past two years, these were royal accommodations for us.

I went up to the attic. The wooden beams reminded me of the ones I had peered through to see the concerts at the Athenaeum. That was perhaps the only thing I could remember with longing from our time in The Fortress.

As the days went on, I went up to the attic a lot more. I told everyone that I was straightening it out, but the real reason was that I wanted to be alone to think. After Catia's return, I came to a decision. I knew that the time had come when our paths would part. I had a promise to keep, and to do so, I had to go another way.

When we started telling her our experiences, I realized how many things had happened since that day I got off the train in the center of Bucharest. We had a hard time summing everything up. When we excitedly told her what happened to us, each of us remembered things differently. I realized that, despite all we had gone through, we had stayed together, and that was special to me.

When Gabriel and Maria entered the house, I recognized

him as the old man who had driven us away from the house when Daniel and I first came there. However, it was Maria who drew my attention. Her graying hair, green eyes, her sweet smile and her white dress with thin brown and gray stripes reminded me of my mother. I immediately felt an ache in my heart.

Gabriel had a serious expression on his face. He had shorts on, and a blue shirt, and his skin was bronzed from the work in the fields. He wore thick black-rimmed glasses, his eyebrows were thick and gray, and the color of his thinning hair was a mix of gray and white.

Their daughter Zsuzsika had lush, shiny brown hair arranged in a braid with a pink ribbon. She wore a flowery blue dress, and was excited to meet us all.

When Lizica, Lili, and Dinu saw her, they all went straight to her room, and since then they were inseparable.

From that day on, the children went back and forth between the two houses. This worried Clara and Constantin a bit, because the children were outside more often, but on the other hand, the kids had more to occupy them, and they ate with Gabriel and Maria too, which helped a lot. It was not easy to feed eleven hungry mouths. Constantin would leave early in the morning for the center of Bucharest and return long after the sun had gone down. Sometimes days passed by without our seeing him. Many nights I would be lying awake on the mattress and hear him coming up the stairs, going toward his bedroom.

He made sure to always come back with things in his sack for us, even if it wasn't much. Sometimes it was vegetables or even books to help us in our learning and reading. He brought seeds to plant, so we were all busy tending the garden. Clara knew how to make real dinners out of the little we had. Gabriel and Maria's dedication, to each other and to us, was amazing. Just like Constantin and Clara, they made us all feel like we were their own children.

Most of all, I was happy for Daniel. Catia had come back into his life and the pair were always together. I saw how happy he was, and maybe that made it easier for me to make a decision.

I would have to talk to Daniel soon. There was something I needed to tell him...

CHAPTER 18

Catia's True Story Revealed

Since the day we met Gabriel, Maria, and Zsuzsika, the children had gone back and forth between the two houses. This worried my parents, so they asked us to try not to walk outside between the houses during the day, and if we did, we should not go alone, but always together.

Early one morning I was sitting on the stone wall Gabriel had built near his house, waiting for Catia. She had gone to get the water buckets, as we wanted to go and bring water from the well for both the houses.

Gabriel went out to gather wood for the stove, and I took the opportunity to ask him something that had been bothering me.

"Gabriel, I wanted to ask you something."

"Yes, Daniel."

"When Nelu and I saw you that time we came, you said that they had killed everyone in the house... I know you protected Catia, but what about her parents? Catia told us something different..."

"Sometimes you keep things to yourself to protect someone, but as time passes, you regret it."

"What do you mean, Gabriel?"

"Catia didn't tell you everything that happened since she came here, because there were things she didn't know. The day her parents disappeared, we split up into three groups and started searching in the grove. I was afraid of what we were going to find, so I sent Catia in the opposite direction of where I was looking. In the field, I found the kerchief Adela had had wrapped around her head, and I understood that this was the direction we should go in. It led into the woods. I called one of the men who worked for me, who had volunteered to help that night, and I asked him to take Zsuzsika home and then come back. I went further into the woods and soon I found them."

"Catia's parents?"

"Yes, Adela and Emil. On the ground, bloodied, brutalized, their clothes torn to shreds… it was one of the worst things I had ever seen, and I had already been through a war. My worker came back from the house. I told him to go back and fetch two hoes, and he did. All that night we dug. Two graves - and we put a marker on them. I could not tell Catia. She had tried so hard to find them. She still had hope, and I could not break her heart. Maria, my worker, and me were the only ones to know about it. I didn't think it would turn out like this, but the first person I ever told about what happened to her parents is you."

Gabriel spoke very little. He was a quiet, sorrowful man, given to melancholy. The wrinkles on the sides of his eyes revealed that he had gone through a great deal in his life, and maybe that was why he did not like to talk. When he told me the story of Catia's parents, I was surprised and shocked. At first, I didn't understand why he had chosen to share this secret with me, but gradually I understood. He knew he was wrong not to tell Catia the truth, and he hoped that I could.

"One day when you are both in the forest - I know you go there a lot - she will see the grave marker. When that happens, I want her to be with someone who cares for her as much as I do."

From the moment Gabriel told me the story, whenever Catia and I approached the forest, I found some excuse to change direction. I knew I would have to take her there one day, but I kept putting it off, time after time.

Lizica and Dinu became part of Gabriel and Maria's household. The feelings of affection were mutual. Catia's house was visited mainly to take care of the garden that thrived with lots of flowers and vegetables. Gabriel and Maria saw in Lizica and Dinu in particular, and the rest of the children in general, an opportunity to invest their energy in educating young people who very much needed their love and a guiding hand.

As part of the division of labor, Nicu and Doru were responsible for carrying out regular patrols around the house to make sure no one suspicious approached, and at night they informed every one of my father's return so we would not panic. Everyone had a hand in the housework - cleaning, washing dishes, carrying buckets of water from the well, and working in the field with Gabriel and Maria. My mother had taken Rita in hand, and she had finally tamed her wild hair. Gabriel and Maria lent her clothes, and suddenly, before our eyes, the street girl with wild hair had turned into a lovely young woman. Mitu was given new glasses to replace the scratched and patched up glasses he wore. Nicu and Doru got clean clothes and short haircuts. They looked more mature and better groomed than the mischievous youngsters we knew. We had become one big family, one that would be preserved forever.

We were all so busy we could not see the change my mother

and father had undergone. They were concerned again, less about the children – who were now also under the care of Gabriel and Maria - but more about the danger still hovering over us in the wake of the Nazi regime. My parents set before themselves a task I was not aware of: to leave Romania as soon as possible.

One day when I was walking with Catia, I lost my sense of time and direction, as I often did when I was with her, only this time I didn't notice that we had entered the forest and continued across it.

"Look, Daniel!"

She said pointing to two wooden stakes stuck in the ground in a clearing in the woods.

The poles were three feet high and three feet apart, stuck in the ground and covered with fallen leaves. When I realized what they were, I went pale. I wanted to take Catia and go back, but it was too late. She was a step ahead of me in everything, and now she was approaching one of the stakes and touching it.

"What are these doing here?"

Without a good answer, I said the only thing that came to mind so as not to give away the truth.

"What do you think they're doing here?"

"I think it's some kind of marking, there's something here. We have to pull them out and dig." Before she even finished the sentence, she was kicking the stake. I could not watch; I knew I had to stop her, to do something before it was too late.

"Catia, maybe we shouldn't touch them. We're far from home, and if you keep making that noise with the stake, someone may hear us. We should go back because..."

"Go back?" she said, and went on pounding, even more

forcefully when she felt her task threatened. "Don't be silly, there's no one here, it's deserted and no one can hear us."

"That's exactly why we need to be closer to home."

"I want to see what's here, with or without you, but if you're a gentleman, come help."

"Catia, stop!"

Catia continued banging at the stake until the ground began to loosen under it. I went to her quickly, hugged her from the back and moved her aside.

"Stop."

"Why should I stop?" She was more determined than ever. "What is it, are you hiding something from me, do you know what's in here?"

"Catia... It's not what is here, it is who…"

At that moment, she stepped back and looked at the wooden stakes. One was inscribed with an "A" and the other with an "E".

I did not know how to tell her. How do you tell someone you love the worst of all possible things?

"These letters are exactly what you think."

"What... what are you talking about... what do you mean?"

Tears began streaming down Catia's cheeks.

She dove at me and began pounding me on the chest.

"Do you think it's funny?! Do you know what you're making me think?"

"Yes…I do."

"Stop it right now! It's not funny, I have to see, I have to..."

She kneeled down toward one of the graves and began digging with her hands. I moved quickly to her and held her so she could not move her arms.

"Leave me alone, I have to find out!"

"Catia, stop!" She struggled hard to free herself from my grip but I would not let go of her. Finally, she got loose and continued digging.

"Catia…" I pulled her face to me and peered deeply into her eyes.

"Stop. It's them, Emil and Adela. Gabriel buried them here himself."

I did not have time to finish the sentence. Catia collapsed on the mound of autumn leaves, screaming and crying.

"It can't be! He said… they would come back!"

I lay next to her and hugged her.

"Gabriel wanted to tell you, but he couldn't…and neither could I."

"How long have you known this, how long have they been here?"

"Gabriel told me last week. They've been here since the night your house was looted."

She lay flat, unmoving, on the graves of her mother and father.

"How could you not tell me they were here? I've been searching for them for so long, so long… I hoped they'd come back, and all the time they were here, in the ground, alone!" She stroked the fallen leaves on the graves. "Mama… Tata," and the tears kept raining down her cheeks.

She laid her head on the ground and spread her hands on the fallen leaves, as if trying to give them one final, loving hug.

"Mama… Tata," her voice became a whisper, and she repeated the words over and over.

I just lay there and held her. I embraced her without a word until she stopped whispering, but the tears continued to fall, all on their own. I held her tightly until she was still, her hands fingering the fallen leaves. And so we lay there in silence together.

"Mother and father."

All I could do was stay with her, hugging her. Nothing could tear her away from that sorrowful clearing among the trees, and we remained lying there all that day.

Later, I opened my eyes. Autumn leaves brushed against my face. A light breeze had choreographed a momentary dance of fallen leaves in front of me. Catia was no longer in my arms. She was on her knees beside the graves, smoothing and straightening the earth over them, in total silence.

I stood up and approached her cautiously, putting my hand on her shoulder.

Catia kept on gazing at the fallen leaves she had cleared from her parents' graves.

After a moment of silence, she said, without taking her eyes off the wooden stake that marked the burial place, "Help me clear off the graves."

"Of course."

I got down on my knees and began to clear away leaves from the area around Emil's grave.

After we finished picking up all the fallen leaves in the area, Catia asked me to help her dig a shallow trough in the ground. We dug a small trench that delineated the area where the two stakes were located, on which we placed stones. It was a long time before we could gather enough stones to fill the entire trench. Catia continued to do everything in silence, as did I. I knew there was nothing I could say that would comfort her.

When we were finished placing the stones, Catia stood up. She seemed to be saying a silent prayer as she put her hand on each of the stakes above the graves, one by one. Her head was bowed, her eyes closed and her mouth murmured words I could not perceive.

After she had finished, she opened her eyes and looked up at me.

"Will you take me back to the house now?"

"Of course."

This was the first and the last time that I would have to lead Catia anywhere. I had never seen her so vulnerable. When we got to the house, she went to Gabriel with tear-filled eyes.

"Why, for so long, why didn't you tell me?"

He looked at her silently. As now the moment he knew was coming had arrived.

"I'm sorry, my dear, I should have, I have no excuses to make."

She looked down at the floor, then ran abruptly upstairs and shut herself up in her room. I started to follow her, but Gabriel grabbed my shoulder and stopped me.

"Let her be alone for now, Daniel. For someone to share his grief, he must first accept it himself. Thank you, Daniel, for your courage. You were able to do what I could not."

I nodded in agreement, but it wasn't comforting in light of Catia's condition.

"I'm going home, I'll come and see how she is later."

But I did not go back that night. Instead, I lay on my mattress tossing and turning, unable to sleep from thinking of her. I knew she was awake too, and I knew I had to let her be. I remembered what Gabriel had said, and he was right.

CHAPTER 19

Nelu's Decision

At first, I did not want to tell the others, but the change in Catia's behavior was obvious. So I preferred to tell them and ask them not to question her about it, to give her time and space to recover.

Catia barely said a word the first few days, but slowly, she started talking to us, even smiling from time to time, but there was sadness in her eyes, even when she smiled. I knew it was something only time could heal. But this kind of pain never heals completely, it only fades. Every day Catia would go to the graves and clean off the fallen leaves. Sometimes I would see her going and suggest I go with her, and she would agree. Sometimes I would see her from afar and let her go alone. It was when Catia began to recover that I began to notice changes taking place around me. My parents seemed distant and isolated. Nelu was never around, Mitu and Rita were closer than ever. Things that were going to affect the future of us all were happening around me without my noticing.

One day I woke up early and went down to the living room while Catia was still asleep. I met Nelu in the kitchen. I felt a need to apologize to him because I had disappeared in the past weeks. I thought he had isolated himself because I had not been there for him.

"Nelu, is everything all right?"

"Yes, everything is all right, Daniel. How about you and Catia?"

"About that, Nelu, I wanted to tell you... maybe we haven't been able to talk lately, but... I—"

Nelu interrupted the blurb of unspoken words coming out of my mouth.

"I can't begin to understand how she feels. It's a tough time for her, and she is lucky to have you. I'm glad you're helping her to recover. She's looking better now."

I was relieved that Nelu wasn't angry with me. I had forgotten he was more mature than he looked.

There was silence. Then:

"Daniel, there's something I need to tell you." He looked more serious than ever. "No one is happier than I am that we are here. Your parents are wonderful, Gabriel and Maria are too, Catia is back, and for now, we are safe. You have been terrific, but…"

"But what, Nelu?"

"Do you remember what I told you about why I always wear the cap on my head?"

The fact was I had forgotten Nelu's personal story until he mentioned his cap.

"Yes," I replied.

"Daniel, I have to leave, I have a mission to complete, and I cannot do it while I'm here. I was ready to get up and go, but I had to talk to you first.

I sympathized with him. I understood. However, at that moment, it was like a knife in my heart. I could not imagine how I could deal with what was to come if Nelu was not at my side. I wanted to tell him to stop and think; tell him we had to stay together. I wanted to tell him about all the things we would do with our longed-for freedom after the war was over. I wanted to persuade him to stay, but I knew he had a private war to win, and he had to do it alone. When there is conflict between heart and mind, the heart wins out. You can influence the mind, but not the heart. Each one of us had to fight his own war, and take different paths.

"I understand, Nelu. You don't know how painful it is for me to say this, but I understand."

"Understand what?" came Catia's voice. She had woken up and come down to the kitchen.

She stood looking at Nelu.

"You want to leave, right?"

"Yes, Catia, I have... things I have to take care of, things that were waiting for me to do even before the beginning of the war."

Catia put her hand on his shoulder.

"And you feel it is the right thing to do?"

"Yes."

"Then you must do it."

We spent the whole day together from start to finish. Nelu made sure to talk with everyone. He didn't tell them what he had told us, but he parted from them in his own way, without sharing his secret.

In the early morning, he was ready. I went to the door with him. Catia was waiting outside.

Nelu stood in the doorway holding a rucksack that had a little food in it, just as he had done three years before. Determined to complete his task, but this time equipped with the strength and ability he had gained over the years. He hugged us for a long time and then left. For a moment, he turned back to us. Then he bowed his head and touched his cap with his thumb and forefinger.

"Don't forget you owe me a concert at the Athenaeum," he said, smiling.

"It's a deal."

As I saw him starting to walk away, I felt part of me being torn away. I suddenly understood I might never see him again. Perhaps our ways would part forever, and as I watched him move off, I wanted to tell him that I had the privilege of seeing the world through his eyes, and that it had changed me. I wanted to thank him for so many things I did not have time to thank him for. I wanted to say goodbye one last time. I started running after him before he disappeared over the horizon and grabbed him by the shoulder. He turned.

"We each have a war to fight, but promise me, Nelu, promise me that in the end, we will meet, triumphant."

"I promise."

We embraced for the last time.

***

Catia continued to visit the graves every day and clear the leaves and dirt away. From time to time, she would gather flowers from the fields and place them on the graves. Once, I was near her as she stood silently by the graves. Tears fell down her cheeks. I moved closer and hugged her. Her head was on my chest.

"Daniel, take me away from here."

"Let's go then."

"I mean for good, Daniel. I can't bear the sorrow."

I hugged her tight, but I didn't know if we would ever be able to leave.

"It will be all right, I will always be here for you."

I accompanied Catia to Maria and Gabriel's house and returned to our house. I saw my father and mother whispering together in the kitchen. As soon as I came in, they went silent.

"Dad," I said, "I know you're hiding something from us, how long are you going to do that? You have to talk to us."

"You're right, Daniel," my father said.

"I know you're trying to take care of us, but the time has come for you to tell me the truth, I can handle it."

He looked at my mother, who nodded, and looked back at me. He surveyed the room around him to make sure no one else was listening.

"You have to promise you will not say a word of what I am telling you now to anyone, not even Catia and Lili."

The seriousness of his tone surprised me, but I nodded without hesitation.

"The situation is very difficult, Daniel. I am in Bucharest every day, and I see it getting worse and worse. You hear a lot of talk in the market, you hear about mass killings of Jews in Bessarabia and Bukovina, deportation to labor camps in Transnistria, deportation of the Jews in Transylvania to labor camps in Ukraine."

"What are you trying to say?"

"I'm trying to say, Daniel, that we are not safe here."

"Not safe? But we are far enough from Bucharest."

"No, Daniel... I am talking about all of Romania—"

"I don't understand," I interrupted. "So why do we sit and do nothing? We can arm ourselves so next time they come, we will be ready!"

"You are right. We must fight our war, but this is not the time, nor the place, and we will not endanger the lives of the children because of our actions."

"They are no longer children, Father, and they will fight alongside us."

"I have no doubt, and that's why we had to find another way: for me, Daniel, they are still children, they are all like my children. I am in contact with some people in Bucharest, friends, activists. There are attempts to escape from the hands of the Nazis by sea."

"What are you talking about, to escape where?"

"To Palestine, my son, to Palestine, the Land of Israel."

Up to that moment, the Land of Israel was a wonderful place that existed only in the stories our parents told us. A place we might one day see, but in reality we were years away from that dream. Despite the fact that our current lives had been crazy in recent years, I did not expect to hear anything like that from my father. I was sure the plan was to stay in hiding until the war was over. Yet I knew that everything my father had said was true, and that we had to prepare ourselves.

"There are all kinds of arrangements that have to be made, but it's important for me to make you understand that we cannot stay here, we must leave before it's too late. Remember that our family and Catia are Jews, and the others have a greater chance of surviving without us. Until we leave, we are in danger here, and we endanger them as well."

"Shouldn't we all sit down and decide this together?"

"No, Daniel. This is not their decision to make. You have to realize that you, Lili, Catia, your mother and I will be hunted first if they come here. The others may survive, but we will not... Do you understand, Daniel? No one can know about this until we have exact plans for our escape."

It was hard keeping it secret from the others, but my father and my mother trusted me, and more importantly, I knew that I might put everyone else in danger, so I said nothing.

I learned that the people my father was in contact with in Bucharest were activists in the Zionist movement. They told my father about the Jews of Transylvania, among them Jews of my father's hometown, Oradea, who had been taken en masse to labor camps. They also heard that there was a secret decision made by the British government that would allow Jews to reach Turkey and then continue the journey to Palestine. If that was true, this was our opportunity. There would be no other. It was a huge risk but one that we had to take, without hesitation.

My parents gave our details to the activists and waited for word from them for our next move.

In time, we told Catia and Lili as well. We could not hide from them the fact that we planned to leave. But still, we couldn't tell the others.

Before long, my father came back from the market with more details. The activists had bought a ship that would depart from Constanţa (Costantsa), a port city in Romania on the Black Sea, about 200 kilometers east of Bucharest. "The route follows the Danube," my father repeated what one of the activists had told him. Despite the rumors that the Germans had sunk some ships that tried to flee Romania by sea, we were going ahead with it. There was no other option.

In normal times, the road to Constanţa took no more than a day, but when you have to stay off main roads and travel much of the way on foot, in secret, it would take at least three days to get there. It was time to tell everyone.

The first ones to hear of our decision were Gabriel and Maria. They had to be told that the responsibility for all the children would pass to them. My father and I gathered the children in Catia's living room: Lizica, Dinu, Mitu, Doru, Nicu, and Rita. Everyone looked at us curiously and waited. It was going to be harder than I thought. I looked into their eyes, but the words would not come, so my father began to speak for me.

"We have something important to tell you, and I need you to listen to my words all the way to the end. It will not be easy for me to say this, so please wait for me to finish if you have something to say."

When they all saw his somber expression, they fell silent.

"As you know, although all our lives have been in danger for a long time, mine, Lili's, Catia's, Daniel's and Clara's are in greater danger because we are Jews. The Germans have been hunting us down and persecuting us in Romania for a long while.

"What do you mean, 'persecuting'?" asked Lizica.

"I mean that they want to hurt us because of our Jewish origin, Lizica."

"I don't understand."

"Neither do we," replied my father, and put his hand on her shoulder. "Neither do we..."

He went on.

"All this time we have been with you, we have become like one family, but at the same time, the fact that we are here puts you in great danger, and we must move on. We must go our own way."

"No!" Lizica had grasped the meaning of the words. "You can't go!" She ran and wrapped her little arms around my father's waist. "Stay here! We'll protect you!"

Her reaction brought tears to our eyes. I quickly wiped them away. It was not the time to break down, everyone was distressed enough without that.

My father leaned toward Lizica, looked at her little face and said, "We must be brave now, my dear Lizica. I need you to promise me something." He looked up at all the children and said, "I need you all to promise me something. You must keep safe; guard the house, yourselves, and Maria and Gabriel, all of you, until we can come back. Can I ask you to do that? If I feel you are going to give up, we won't be able to succeed ourselves."

"Is there no other way? If there isn't, then we could come with you!" Mitu said.

"There is no other way, and we cannot take you with us. We can't endanger you," answered my father.

The children all accepted this in silence, and nodded.

Only Lizica screamed, "No, no! You are not really going, are you, Daniel?"

"We need you all to do this for us," concluded my father.

No eyes were dry, but no one spoke. The silence in the room seemed an eternity.

Nicu went over to my father, put his hand on his shoulder and looked at us. We saw in his eyes all we had been through, all we had shared, the wonderful friendship that we had built. In all the madness of the times, we had become brothers.

"We promise the Lupescu family and Catia that we will protect the house, because no matter where we live, for us and for you, this is our fortress, and we are the Knights of The Fortress. We will not let it fall into the hands of the enemy."

We took him in our arms, and that is when I realized how

much he had grown. He was already taller than I and his arms were thicker than mine. He hugged us warmly, as he had never done before, and after a few seconds, Doru, Rita, Dinu and Mitu joined him. Only Lizica stood crying from behind. My father stretched out his hand to her, but she refused to join us and ran to her room. I wanted to go after her, but my father grabbed me.

"Let her be, Daniel, she needs time."

We stood embracing; the final embrace of the extended family, and it gave us all the strength to continue. We knew that our ways would be separate, but our struggle was one.

For the next few days, we waited anxiously for my father to come back from the market and tell us we were on our way. He had to get final confirmation of the departure date so we could leave, but the activists did not contact him. Each day seemed longer than the last. We were ready to go but had to be patient. We used our remaining time to enjoy being with everyone, and it is precisely this period I remember most. For all we knew, these were our last moments, and we did almost everything we could together.

Finally, after four days, the activists made contact with my father.

In the first days of November, 1942 a ship would sail from Constanța and take us to Turkey. From there we would continue by train to Palestine.

Our few possessions were ready for the journey. We were asked to take as little as possible to make the journey easier. At the time, my thoughts were not about what I was going to take with me, but about what I was leaving behind. It was a journey into the unknown, and I knew that I was leaving my family. After Nelu had left, I did not think I would have to part from the other children. I was still struggling with wanting to stay with them or even take them with us, but I knew we were putting them at risk, so I did not say a word.

My father spoke to Nicu about his being the oldest in the group, and that he would have to take responsibility. I knew he would help Maria and Gabriel. I trusted him, I trusted all of them. That made it easier on me, for I knew they would be safe.

My mind wandered over everything I was leaving behind and I wondered what the journey would bring. In our days in The Fortress in Bucharest, we thought things would improve, and we still believed that when we moved to Catia's house. Yet all this time the situation had only deteriorated and we had to go on another journey, this time the most dangerous of them all, and the odds seemed to be against us. I prayed each day that luck would remain on our side, but prepared for the worst.

CHAPTER 20

The Momentous Journey

By the end of September, the activists sent my father final word that the ship would sail November 4th. That meant we had to set out at dawn on the 1st of November. We learned that the ship had been engaged by local authorities and would leave at night. On the first leg of the journey, until we got to the ship, we were to travel with the activists from the Zionist movement. Because of strict security checks by the regime, we were to stay off the main roads and travel on foot. The fateful hour arrived. Everyone was there for our departure except Lizica, who was still angry. We hugged the others, and when we saw that Lizica wasn't there, we went up to the top floor to look for her. She had closed herself in one of the rooms. My father knocked on and asked to come in. When we opened the door, we saw Lizica sitting in a corner of the room, furrowing her brow. My father got down on his knees to be at eye level with her.

"Lizica dear, I know you're angry, and that you think we can stay here and we have chosen to leave. Believe me, dear, we must go, and that is the only reason we are leaving you."

"But why can't you stay, you are just giving up!"

"I'll never give up on you. You are angry now that we have

to part, but one day you will understand. I love you, my little flower." He kissed her on the forehead, but she did not respond. She lowered her head towards her knees. Father got up and walked toward the door where the rest of us were standing. I saw in his eyes how painful it was for him to leave her like that. We went back to the door and said goodbye for the last time - and we started walking away. Suddenly, my father stopped. I didn't know why, but we all stopped walking as well. Then we heard a sound coming from the house. A voice grew louder and it became clear who it was coming from.

"*Unchiu! Unchiu!*[21]" My father turned around as Lizica ran out of the house toward him. He threw his sack on the ground, knelt down, and spread his arms for her. Lizica jumped on him and he gathered her up in his arms and stood up. They remained in an embrace for several moments.

"Thank you, my little flower, for coming to say good-bye." We all hugged Lizica and when Nicu came to escort her back home, we continued on our way.

Part of our hearts remained behind in the house that day with the children. Already in our first steps away, we felt how hard it would be without them. But there was no going back; we had embarked on the most important journey of our lives.

---

21   *Unchiu* = Uncle

CHAPTER 21

Nelu

When I was little, I didn't grasp the true meaning of the step I was going to take as I stood at the door of the house and looked back at my mother one final time. My feet seemed not to want to support me, but I knew what I had to do. Years Later, when I stood at Catia's doorstep, it was the same thing; except this time, I understood. This time again my legs almost failed me, but I was determined. I left full of hope, and yet my heart ached. I knew I would not see them again for a long time. I made an effort to smile so that they would not see how hard it was for me. I hugged Daniel one last time and walked off.

I returned to my solitude in Bucharest. It had been so long since I had first left home, but now I was no longer the lost child I was then. This time I had an important goal; a promise I had to keep. I arrived at Alex's cofetarie at noon.

Alex was excited to see me and hugged me warmly.

"Nelu! I can't believe what a fine young man you have become! Look at you!"

I was not sure he would remember me, and if he did, he might be angry with me for leaving without a word those years ago. However, from the first moment he saw me, he greeted my return with affection.

We sat in the cofetarie and I told him everything that had happened to me since I left. I explained that I had not returned because I was afraid at first, but then I was simply ashamed to show my face because I had run away.

"It doesn't matter, Nelu, as long as you're here, sound and healthy, that's more important."

"Are you still looking for people to work?"

"If you stay here this time, then, yes," he smiled, twirling his long mustache.

I put my sack behind the counter and started my job.

At the end of the day, Alex came up to me.

"Nelu, do you have anywhere to stay?"

"Don't worry," I told him, "I'll manage."

"Come on, help me close up." As he arranged the metal mesh that protected the display, he continued, "You kids today, you kill me with your stubbornness. You come with me now, and I don't care what you say, you sleep at my house."

I smiled.

"I don't feel right coming like this without notice."

"Stop the nonsense; you're like a member of the household."

Alex led the way, and we started walking.

"Listen Nelu, I live in a big apartment with only my wife and daughter. We have an extra room that we occasionally rent out. I have to say, I have never rented to one of my employees, but I'll make an exception in your case – I'll deduct the rent from your wages, and if you help with the household chores, I will take less off."

I wanted to say something, but before I could open my mouth, he was patting me on the shoulder.

"Good, so the matter is settled."

We walked about three blocks until we reached a beautiful

three-story building. A staircase led to the front door entrance. We entered the first apartment on the right.

The apartment was as welcoming and worm as Alex's character. Inside the apartment was a living room with two sofas and an armchair arranged around a low wooden table trimmed with carving along the edges. The sofas and the armchair were made of dark wood with a beige-colored backrest, decorated with a beautiful pink and blue bouquet of flowers. The cushions were sectioned into eight squares. White curtains with delicate floral prints covered the windows.

Alex's wife came into the living room and he introduced me: "This is Nelu. You remember him, he worked for me when he was a boy, and now that he is back at the cofetarie, I want to rent him our spare room. Nelu, this is Luci, my wife."

"With your permission, Mrs. Eminescu, if it's all right... I would like to rent a room in your apartment."

Luci smiled at me.

"Any friend of Alex is a friend of the family. You are a polite young man, and I have no problem having nice, polite people in the apartment."

I asked Alex again.

"Don't worry, worst comes to worst I'll sleep on the sofa," and he laughed. When he saw I didn't understand the joke, he looked at me and said "when you're married, you'll understand".

"Come into the living room for some tea."

We sat in the living room, drinking tea and enjoying pastries from the cofetarie. I told Alex and Luci about my experiences, until at one point Alex decided it was time for bed.

"Well now, let's let the boy sleep, he must be tired," he said, and winked at me. I was very tired, no doubt of that, and I was glad to retire to my room. It had a bed and a dresser, and even a work desk and a chair. That was plenty for me.

The next day, Alex knocked on my door to let me know that breakfast would be in a few minutes. I got up, dressed quickly, and went to the living room. At the table sat a beautiful girl with big blue eyes, her hair smooth and black, flowing over her shoulders.

"Nelu, this is Laura, my daughter."

"Hello, Nelu."

I smiled awkwardly and shook her hand.

Alex's family treated me as one of the family. After only a week, I felt like I had been living with them for years.

I opened the cofetarie with Alex every day at sunrise, so that everything would be ready for the customers in the morning, and at night we would close it together and return home. Laura would visit us almost every day, and when there were no customers, we would sit and talk. One day after she had gone, Alex patted me on the back and smiled.

"I don't remember Laura visiting me so much when I was here alone without help."

I smiled, embarrassed.

The weeks and months passed, and every so often, I would send a letter to my house in the village, hoping that my sister Anna would receive it. I had done that even when I was in The Fortress, but because I did not have much money, I could not send them often.

"I want you to know I haven't forgotten, and I will return as I promised..."

I also sent letters to Gabriel and Maria to say that I was fine and to ask it they were safe.

I often thought about everyone there before I fell asleep. I hoped they are all alright, wherever they are.

***

The war ended, and Romania was now under the rule of the Red Army - Communism. The devastation of the war was evident in Bucharest, but the cofetarie had remained standing. The customers differed from time to time, but the cofetarie was always full. Some things do not change. The way Alex ran the place and his generous manner, made people loyally come back.

It was not long before Alex let me work the cash register. I felt honored that he trusted me, and I invested all my energy into my work. We changed the signs in the display cases, adjusted prices to meet the needs and capacity of our customers according to changing times, and most of all, we served them with a smile and with all our hearts, just as Alex had always done.

"You have a talent for these things, son" he said to me.

The number of clients in the cofetarie was increasing, and Alex and his family were caring for me, making me feel part of a family again… and my connection with Laura grew closer.

During this time, I was able to save most of my salary. Apart from the letters, I hardly spent anything. It had been a little over six months, but now, finally, I had enough to go on the mission I had been planning for years.

A few weeks earlier, I had started looking for an apartment suitable for my budget, and luckily, I found one not far from the *cofetarie*. It was small and unfurnished, but it was a start. This would be the apartment where I could bring my mother and sister.

I spoke to Alex that week at home.

"Alex, I want to thank you for everything you have done for

me, not only now, but also when I was a child..."

"You don't have to thank me, Nelu, and besides, you're still a child," he said, smiling at me.

"As you know I've been looking around for an apartment lately and... I'm going to rent one, not because I don't want to stay here anymore, on the contrary, you're like family to me, you're wonderful to me... I just want to bring my mother and sister from the village to live with me. Tomorrow morning I won't go with you to work, but I promise to return, I'm not running away any more!"

Alex looked at me silently for a moment. The expression on his face changed, astonishingly to understanding, and before I found the right words to continue explaining to him, he asked me:

"Is this related to what you told us about your family?"

"Yes."

"I'm a great believer in closing loose ends, so go do it. Don't worry, we'll wait for you."

I was relieved he understood, but I also had to tell Laura. I spoke to her that evening and asked her to wait for me. I promised her I would be back, and except for my living in another apartment, nothing would change.

On Friday, I set out.

After so many years, back to my mother's house... and my father's...

CHAPTER 22

Daniel

We set out at night, moving together in the fields alongside the road. It was early November, and winter chill accompanied us all throughout the march. We were wrapped in coats with layers of clothing beneath. After about two hours of walking, we met up with the activists my father had been in contact with, and they led the rest of the way. One of them, Manuel, was a burly man with gray hair and mustache. He wore two jackets that were full of holes. I wondered how they had protected him from the bitter cold of the night, because our clothes certainly had not. The second man, Ilie, was younger and thinner. His bushy hair showed through the hood of his coat, which was a few sizes too large for him. Along the way, four more people joined us. They had escaped from Bessarabia, an elderly couple with two children, A boy named Viorel and a girl named Rodica. They were Lili's age. Their light colored hair was hidden under thick woolen caps and their coats looked particularly thick as well. The couple left them in the care of Manuel and Ilie and parted ways from us. The children's parents had managed to give them to the elderly couple just before they were caught and taken away. The elderly couple had hidden them, but now they couldn't risk their safety anymore. The children wept softly. This was the second time that they had been taken from those they love and trust. Two other young men joined us a few miles down the road, Liviu and Radu. They had escaped the pogrom in Iasi, ordered by Ion Antonescu's forces and the German Army's 30th Infantry Division. Antonescu himself stated, "I am in favor of expelling the Jews from Bessarabia and [Northern] Bukovina to the other side of the border. There is nothing for them here and I don't mind if history calls us barbarians… There has never been a time more suitable in our history to get rid of the Jews, and if necessary, you are to make use of machine guns against them."

We continued on almost nonstop over hills and alongside the forest, and only towards the end of the night did we stop to rest for a few hours. At dawn, we continued until we reached the road.

We walked along the road near the forest. Each time Ilie and Manuel thought they heard a car, they signaled us to go in among the trees, where we stayed hiding until the car passed. They could not take any chances. After a few more hours, they stopped and started arguing. I thought they were looking for something, but it turned out they were waiting. The despair and worry were evident in their faces. Suddenly we heard a noise. The activists again ordered us to hide among the trees, and we hurried to do as they said. It was a truck, and it came closer until it neared the area where we were hiding, then it slowed and finally stopped.

It seemed they had spotted us. We were not well hidden, and now we would have to pay the price. I was frightened. Suddenly, Ilie and Manuel came out from behind the trees and signaled to the truck where the rest of us were. Could all of this be a trap? The truck began to inch toward us. Manuel approached them and Ilie went toward us. He laid a hand on my father's shoulder.

"This is our ride to Constanța."

Manuel hurried to the truck and greeted the driver and the young man sitting next to him. He came down, shook Manuel's hand, and Manuel put an envelope in his hand. The man put it in his coat pocket and went to the back of the truck. At the same time, Ilie signaled us to come out of hiding and approach the truck.

"Come on, get on."

They opened the door and got us on one by one. Ilie went up with us, but Manuel did not join us. The truck was loaded with crates. We had to climb over them to get to a place where we could hide. They brought us tarps to cover ourselves with, so we could not be seen if the truck was stopped at a checkpoint.

We were ready to move. Manuel stood outside and began to close the doors, smiling at us and giving us a last wave of goodbye. I never saw him again, but to this day, I can still picture him waving to us. We settled down into our hiding place and covered ourselves with the tarps. Ilie, the younger activist, knocked on the side of the truck twice, and it started moving.

The truck ride was bumpy and uncomfortable, but better than walking in the freezing cold outside.

We sat in darkness and total silence and tried to fall asleep. Despite the harsh conditions, fatigue overwhelmed us and we slept. I do not know how long I slept, but I woke up when the truck stopped. There were loud voices outside. We had reached a roadblock.

"Open the doors!"

The driver tried to convince the authoritative voice that it was unnecessary, but he insisted.

"Open the doors!"

Ilie checked that we were well covered, and signaled us to remain quiet. The latch on the door began to descend and the doors opened with a shrill creak.

"What do you have here?"

"Crates of potatoes and other vegetables from the farm."

Suddenly the truck began to shake. We heard footsteps... one step, then another step... the man with the authoritative voice had climbed onto the truck and was walking around the crates. I thought he had noticed something odd, and he reached out his hand to grasp the sheet that was covering us when there was a sudden shout from outside.

"There's another one coming!"

He dropped the corner of the sheet. Silence hung in the air for a few crucial seconds, then a sound of footsteps moving away.

"Go on, close the doors and drive off."

We breathed a sigh of relief.

The truck pulled away. It was only after about five minutes that we dared to poke our heads out slowly through the black tarps.

"It's all right," said Ilie, "luck was on our side. I hope we will not need it again. When it gets dark, we will get off the truck and continue on foot."

After the stop at the checkpoint, we weren't able to sleep any more. We sat tense and excited until the truck stopped again. Ilie got out, walked toward the doors and the handle began to descend again. The doors opened. Outside, it was pitch black.

"Faster!" Ilie urged us. "We don't have much time, the truck has to go back on the road before anyone notices that it stopped. We have a long way ahead, but if we keep up the pace we can rest before the last leg of the journey."

Ilie led us down a dirt road that split off from the main road and led into a wooded area. We walked for a few hours under cover of darkness, each of us with his own thoughts. I glanced around, and for a moment, it seemed to me that one of the boys was Nelu. I smiled to myself. I wished Nelu was here with me... I wished they all were here...

We reached a clearing, where we could lay down some sheets and try to sleep. We drank from the water bottles we had with us. Ilie carried a ten-gallon can on his back and occasionally filled the empty bottles. We ate some of the vegetables and bread, because we did not know how long it would be before we could rest again. I wanted to make a bonfire to warm us up. We were in an isolated area, so I thought it would be all right. Ilie saw me gathering stones and beginning to lay twigs and branches in the middle of them. He ran over and scattered everything.

"No, sorry, flames can be seen from a distance, and a bonfire would leave fresh traces to show we were here, we can't risk it." He walked away without even waiting for any response.

My father came and stood next to me.

"It's not for nothing that I trust Ilie, he leaves nothing to chance, and that's very likely why not even one of the groups he led was ever caught. If he says it's dangerous, you can believe it."

Despite the night sounds in the forest, we all soon fell asleep. At dawn, I felt a hand on my shoulder, Ilie again.

"Come on, we have to continue if we want to get to Constanța while it's still light."

"That's too early; the ship's leaving at night!" I answered with the insolence of youth. He looked at me for a moment...

"The ship leaves at night, but we'll get there early, and wait at the edge of the forest where it meets the fields near the harbor. When darkness comes, we will cross the fields. If you want to reach the port alive, you should stick to my plan."

It was the hardest part of the journey. We walked all day, trying to keep up with Ilie's pace. We stopped only twice for a few minutes to drink and eat a little, and went on.

"Don't worry," my father said during one of the breaks, 'this will be over soon, and then we can rest, and finally head for the ship, can you smell it? Freedom!" His words and energy cheered us up, especially in light of Ilie's firmness.

We continued walking without complaining or asking for more stops, and as Ilie said, before the evening, we reached the end of the forest. We were elated at the sight of the fields that stretched before us. On the horizon, past the fields, we saw lights.

"See those lights there?" Ilie pointed to them, "The port of Constanța." I moved out of the woods to get a better look, but Ilie stopped me. "No, not a step out of the forest as long as there is daylight, we sit and wait until dark, and only then will it be safe to leave."

"No one is here except us, why not now?"

"That's what my brother thought," Ilie said. "They caught him leading a group not far from here."

"Where is he now?"

"My brother came on all the trips with me, do you see him here?"

We sat at the edge of the forest among the trees and waited. The wait was tedious, but at least we could rest.

Darkness fell. Ilie waited another hour and then ordered us to go into the fields. We began to cross them, and this was the first time I could see the sky. It was bright and full of stars. I suddenly remembered the promise I had made to Lili... "See if you can find the Pegasus constellation, Lili," I smiled at her, and she, with glittering eyes, stopped and began searching the sky. I knew Ilie would get angry if there was a delay, so I pointed northwest with my finger, and she recognized it. The sky was clear and glowing, uninterrupted by city or village lights. The scene was spectacular.

"I told you Lili; I promised you we'd be free under the night sky and see the constellation!" I smiled at her and put my arm on her shoulder. We were on the road to freedom.

I had never seen a harbor, never seen the sea. It was night, but still, the enormous vista that opened up before us and the intense emotions we felt left us all with mouths agape.

A very wide wooden structure was the base for ships anchored nearby. Alone, one by one, they calmly sat upon the silent waves of the night. Only one ship was attached to the dock where people were boarding. I stopped for a moment and marveled at its size. A bridge of wooden planks were joined by rope to a dock, and at the head of the bridge stood a man that checked people, allowing them to board.

"Friends," said Ilie, "welcome to your ship."

As I approached the ship, I saw it was old and rickety. Suddenly I was afraid she might sink.

"This is supposed to take us to Istanbul?" my mother asked doubtingly.

"All the way to Istanbul, Mrs. Lupescu, I assure you," Ilie replied decisively.

Little by little, people began to gather on the platform. Groups by groups they came. Two crew members got off the boat and stood by the wooden bridge. They signaled everyone to move forward. Politely and quietly, everyone began to climb onto the bridge and we followed. Ilie said goodbye and hugged my father warmly. I was surprised that it was hard for me to part with him though he had urged us on mercilessly and was tough on us the whole way. But it was thanks to him that we made it. How many such groups had he so peacefully transferred, I wondered, and who will lead us now?

We boarded the ship. We could see that the interior of the ship was also old, dirty, and not well maintained. The sight brought fear back into our hearts. The stern of the ship was similar: one long, covered passageway served as a corridor from which rows of very small cells protruded. One on top of the other. Each cell served as a bed.

The number of people who boarded the ship was larger than I had thought it would be - at least two hundred. We all gathered in the stern, each found a cell to lie in. The passage was crowded and heavily congested. The cold that had accompanied us all during the journey was replaced by the oppressive heat in the stern of the ship.

They hoisted the anchor, and we set sail in the middle of the night.

We were asked to stay in the cells, but I couldn't help myself. I slipped onto the top deck. I wanted to say good-bye to Romania... I stood on deck, the cold wind freezing my bones, but I didn't care. I saw the harbor lights moving farther away and realized I might not see Romania again.

Others came on deck for air because of the stifling heat below. Most of them were turned back in by the crew out of fear that German ships and submarines patrolling the area would see us. Any suspicion, even the smallest, could have doomed the ship. I went back to my cell, but after half an hour I couldn't stand it, so I snuck up onto the deck again, and this time Catia and Lili joined me. As we stood looking at the starry sky, I thought I saw a bright spot on the horizon. A few seconds later a distant line of light appeared on the waves.

"Germans! Germans!" came a shout from one of the crew. "Quick, under cover!" This time there was no need for anyone to tell us to go back down into the ship. The crowd of people on the deck ran along with us into the narrow corridor and disappeared into it. All the lights went out.

"From now on, absolute silence!" A crewmember called out. "There's a German ship nearby..." We all knew what a German ship meant - certain death.

For a long time we waited in tense silence, until a crew-member came, "We got away from the watch dogs."

We breathed a sigh of relief. Applause was heard from all sides and the lights went back on.

For two days, we were at sea. Poor Lili got seasick, and we had to sit with her most of the time.

The ship reached Istanbul in the early morning hours. We were ordered to stay in the stern of the ship until it was anchored at the pier. The dock of Istanbul was larger and more splendid than the pier at Constanţa, with buildings extending all along its length. The activists wasted no time, and immediately after an exchange with the port personnel, we disembarked and started walking to the train station, following the activists.

It was early morning, and though it was a bustling port city, there were few people on the streets. After half an hour, we reached the train station platform. Waiting was nerve racking. The activists divided us into groups so as not to attract attention. Each group counted fifty people. The feeling that the Germans were still after us did not leave us. How can one break free of the fear, that has accompanied him for years, in just a few days?

After a few hours, we were thrilled to hear the rattle and roar of the train coming into the station. The black steam engine's whistle screeched out its arrival. The locomotive gleamed in the sunlight, and steam poured from its turret. The train slowed down until it stopped in front of us on the platform. The men began to climb up and fill the cars.

"We're lucky," one of the activists turned to my father. "We ride a train to freedom, while many of our people ride a train to their deaths." Those words would be forever engraved in my memory.

The locomotive whistled again to announce its departure, and so we began the last leg of our journey to the Land of Israel. The excitement was palpable. The train swung through Turkey's spectacular landscape and, though I was fascinated by the scenery, the trip to Syria and then farther on to Tripoli was long and arduous. The train rumbled on, with minimal stops along the way.

Each passenger had a story to tell on how they had made it to the train. One of the passengers spoke of the line of tracks built by the Turks while they were in control of Palestine. "The Hejaz Railway," he called it. Among those on the train were other families smuggled out of Romania like we were, and there were some passengers that were completely alone. They had lost everything and were able to save only themselves. Others spoke of the significance of immigration to Eretz Israel and the importance of strengthening the Jewish community there. Everyone was full of hope and excitement - finally our fate was in our own hands.

The train stopped in Beirut, Lebanon.

One of the activists turned to us and said excitedly, "Next stop, Palestine!"

CHAPTER 23

Nelu - The Return Home

The train arrived at the station. After so long, so many thoughts and plans, I returned to the village. It looked the same, but if felt different. I think it was me that had changed. A gray village in the heart of the everlasting shades of the green valley. To me, the grayness that accompanied my childhood still cried out from every corner of it.

I walked through the village streets and waved hello to people.

Only one of them recognized me, "Why it's little Nelu, my goodness, how you've grown! Come in, sit down with us!"

"I would like that, but I have to go home first," I smiled.

I walked on, reached the neglected garden outside the house, and went to the door. I gave a light knock and, after a few minutes without a response, a stronger knock. After another minute, the door opened – my father stood in the doorway.

His face had hardly changed except for new and deeper creases on the sides of his eyes. There were the same bloodshot eyes and cheeks flushed with drink, the same penetrating and disparaging look, but with one big difference: this time, his look did not seem threatening, but ridiculous. He was only a little taller than I was, and it was easy to look straight into his eyes. He squinted in the daylight that came through the door.

"Another night of drinking?" I asked.

When his eyes managed to focus, he recognized me.

"Well, look here - look who decided to pay a visit after all these years." The alcohol stench from his mouth sickened me. Nothing had changed.

I stood there in silence.

"So… you think after so long you can just drop by and we'll invite you in, offer you some coffee and cake? You don't live here anymore!"

I remained silent.

"What? They cut out your tongue in Bucharest?" He was waiting for me to look surprised because he knew where I had been, but I gave him no more than a cold stare.

"Oh, yes, you thought I didn't know where you went, but they told me they saw you getting on the train, you bastard! So what do you want now?"

"I want to see how Anna and Elena are." I took a step forward toward the inside of the house. He stood in front of me to block my way.

"You're not welcome here, bastard."

"Get out of my way, you stupid old drunk!" I could no longer control my anger, and it began to take effect. I pushed hard on the door and shoved my father back inside.

I saw Anna on the far left of the living room sitting on the couch, looking at us anxiously. I looked at my father just as he raised his hand toward my face. Years had passed since he had struck me with that hand. Years had passed since he had swung that hand at me, but this was the first time it had been stopped before it got close. I grabbed his hand tightly as it flew through the air. The angry look on his face was replaced by a surprised look I will never forget. He tried to free his hand, but he could not.

"Stupid child! Let go of my hand, or I'll hit you until you bleed!"

I just smiled, still grasping his hand.

"What are you grinning at, you stupid bastard, is this how you treat your father?

"Bastard, I wish I was a bastard, with a father like you."

He clenched his other hand and tried to hit me in the face. I stepped back and he missed and almost fell. It had taken me fourteen years of life to get to this point. In the five years since I had left home, I had dreamed about this moment almost every day. All the anger—the childhood he stole from me, what he did to my mother and my sister, the lives he ruined— all that fury was gathered into an avenging fist that smashed into his face. The strongest punch I could muster. He collapsed unconscious on the floor.

CHAPTER 24

The Journey to Palestine

"Next stop - Palestine!"

Those words sounded like magic. They played melodies in my ears like a work of George Enescu. A smile spread across my face. The last leg of the trip was the longest. We sat glued to the windows, not wanting to miss a speck of the landscape of the Land of Israel. The station in Haifa for me existed only in the moment we would arrive, descend, and feel the earth beneath us. Feel the land of Israel.

In my mind, I saw people cheering at the station, bottles of champagne opening. In my imagination, I saw us being carried off with cries of joy and led directly to a platform where we were given a token of thanks for our journey, with thunderous applause from the astonished crowd.

However, the train stopped at a checkpoint girded by fences and metal grids before it reached Haifa. British soldiers boarded and began asking us questions. Although we tried, we could not understand what they wanted. The activists who knew a little English spoke with them and the soldiers allowed the train to continue.

The train went onward to Haifa, and we saw the sea through its windows. I looked at the thousands of bright spots the sun had created on the water, and forgot about everything – it was only the sea and me.

We reached the last stop – Haifa! We got off the train excitedly and finally the moment we all longed for has arrived. We walked on the soil of Eretz Israel. Some people cried and hugged each other, some cheered, and others got down on their knees and kissed the ground. We had finally reached the land of Israel. It was a moment of indescribable joy.

The concrete platform led to long, white rectangular building with two floors and tiled roofs. There were two towers on the roof. One was a decorated clock tower with a dome that had a strange crescent on its top. The first floor had several entrances, and the upper story, as well as its windows, had arches.

I looked up at the sky – bluer than ever before. The sun washed over me pleasantly and I closed my eyes to feel this moment. The victory, the sense of security. "You're here, you're safe, you're free," it whispered to me. I did not see any fancy buildings and no cheering crowd came to greet us. There were no bottles of champagne and no one lifted me up in the air, but I was happy. At last, after so many years, we were free. We took the first steps in what would later become the State of Israel.

The British soldiers there did not give us much time to enjoy the feeling of freedom. They moved us immediately by train to a detention camp in Atlit, on the Mediterranean coast.

Already at the entrance, we felt apprehensive. A gravel path separated two barbed-wire fences and at the far end stood a black metal iron gate with a watchtower above it. On entry, we were told that the men and women would be separated in the camp. We dreaded a separation, but we had no choice. We hoped that this would be no more than a few days and we could leave, but we did not know what was going to happen to us.

After registration and separation, came the hardest part. We were sprayed with DDT. They 'asked' us to take off our clothes in a disinfecting shed and sprayed us. Although we were told that the spraying was to prevent the transmission of disease, it was a humiliating experience.

The next step was the move to the barracks. The whole camp was packed with long wooden barracks, and my father and I were placed in one of them. Lili, Catia, and my mother were moved to the women's section. The barracks had metal cots spread out in rows along its entire length. They were so close together it was hard to stand between them. This was not the reception we expected, but at least we got regular meals and we could walk around the camp, so we could meet Lili, Catia, and my mother at the fences and exchange experiences.

CHAPTER 25

Joining the British War Effort

After a few days in the camp, we realized we had to do something, or else we would remain there for a long while. Catia and I decided we would enlist in the British Army. It was at the time of General Rommel's invasion of Africa and his advance towards the Middle East. The winds of war were drawing closer. The British began to rely more and more on the local population, and made an effort to harness it to the war effort. Our joining the British Army paved the way for the family to receive certificates of authorization[22] to be released from the camp within days.

Since Jerusalem had become a military center for the growing number of British forces in the Middle East, my parents decided to start their lives anew there, and we all moved to the holy city.

We rode to Jerusalem on a bus for British soldiers and their families. They greeted us with smiles and tried to communicate with us. Though we had little to say, we were relieved to receive such warm gestures. I saw them as heroes because I knew they

---

22   Certificates authorizing immigration into Palestine during the British Mandate period

were fighting the Nazis, which strengthened my desire to join the British forces in the war.

Our first apartment in Israel was in Beit Hakerem neighborhood, in a faded, two-story white building, surrounded by trees and gravel paths. There were few buildings in the area, so the David Yellin teachers' seminar could be seen in the distance. The apartment was empty and small, but it was ours. Beit Hakerem was then a relatively isolated neighborhood far from the center of the city. It was close to the Arab villages of Deir Yassin and Ein Karem, and their residents would often harass us, but we managed to establish and maintain a routine.

On the day we rode the bus to Jerusalem with the British soldiers, I joined the second anti-aircraft artillery unit, where we trained with Italian 20mm cannons and a heavy anti-aircraft machine gun nicknamed "Lewis". After a few months, my unit was sent to protect the Dead Sea Works. I was part of the first Hebrew battery of anti-aircraft guns, which would later become the Israeli Artillery Corps.

Catia was recruited into the Women's Corp in Jerusalem as a clerk, and my mother stayed with Lili in the apartment to deal with the daily civilian life in the new country.

My father used his extensive financial knowledge to help establish additional British camps in various buildings in Jerusalem. In this way, he created the initial connection with the Anglo-Palestine Bank, and later got a job there. Catia and I hardly ever saw each other those days.

Every third weekend I would make my way back to Jerusalem. As if nature was trying to demonstrate the sharp transition from army life to home, when I would get down off the military vehicle in Jerusalem, the cool mountain air of Jerusalem would replace the searing heat of the Dead Sea. Home. Going back to the apartment in Jerusalem after such a long period meant the possibility of seeing Catia and the family again, and that made these weekends very happy ones.

We felt like pioneers, part of the Jewish community in the Land of Israel, and there was no feeling more inspiring than that.

Almost every time we met, we took the time to write letters full of excitement about our life in Israel to Gabriel and Maria, and expressed our concern and hope for the welfare of the cherished people we had left behind.

Time after time, when the letters came back with a Romanian return-to-sender post mark, we were struck with deep sadness, but we never stopped sending those letters. It was perhaps the greatest heartache we suffered in those years, not knowing what had happened to them.

In the absolute solitude of guard duty at the Dead Sea, looking out over the endless landscape of the desert along with the Judean Hills, I would longingly think of the weekend when I would see Catia again, my mother, my father and my sister. Yet my longing for the family I had left behind in Romania was gut wrenching. I thought of them all: Nelu, Doru, Lizica, Dinu, Maria and Gabriel, Zsuzsika, Mitu, Rita, and Nicu. If only I could know they were all right, maybe some of the pain would have been less. Along with that pain were my feelings of guilt for not having taken them with us.

Up to the end of 1942, we guarded the Dead Sea Works. Sometimes we would get a few hours off and we would take a military vehicle to one of the deserted beaches, peel off our uniforms and enter the water. It was easy to become one with nature - to feel the weightlessness, hearing the lulling flow of the water in your ears, and to look up at the sky and the Jordanian mountains. To this day, I go down to the Dead Sea when I want to free myself from the hassle of everyday life. It has this magic, the sense of infinity that allows you to be swallowed up within it.

By the beginning of 1943, my unit was transferred to the Haifa area to protect the refineries and the Stella Maris from aerial bombardments. It was there we were supplied with modern 40mm anti-aircraft guns, manufactured by Beaufort. They held a big party for us to mark the two-year anniversary of the establishment of the Israeli anti-aircraft battery. At the end of 1943, we went by train to Port Said, and from there, to Cyprus. We had a few days off to spend at home before starting training. I took full advantage of them and made Catia my wife. It was one of the happiest weeks of my life and I cherished every minute. There was no telling what would happen when I returned to my unit.

After training in Egypt at Port Said, we transferred to Cyprus to protect Famagusta and the airport at Nicosia. We used to scribble things like "A gift for Hitler" on the artillery shells and hope they would find their mark and indeed, we did a lot of harm.

Only at the end of 1944 did Romania's King Michael request to remove the country from Germany's Axis alliance. Conducător Ion Atonescu refused and was promptly arrested by soldiers of the guard, being replaced as premier by General Constantin Sănătescu, who presided over a national government that declared peace with the Allies and war on Nazi Germany.

It was the news we had all been waiting for back home. I kept writing letters to the family in Jerusalem, not knowing if the news had reached them or not. Later I heard that Ion Antonescu spent those days in custody at a house in Bucharest's Vatra Luminoasă quarter and then handed to the Soviets who transported him to Moscow, together with his deputy Mihai Antonescu, Governor of Transnistria Gheorghe Alexianu, Defense Minister Constantin Pantazi, Gendarmerie Commander Constantin Vasiliu, and Bucharest Police Chief Mircea Elefterescu.

We returned only at the end of 1944. Finally I was able to go back home and reunite with my family. Nazi Germany surrendered in May 1945, bringing the bloody war and all it had symbolized for us to its end. Catia and I were released from our service in the British Army and we all returned to live together in our house in Jerusalem.

As it turned out, Antonescu was interrogated and reputedly tortured, and at some point during this period, he attempted suicide in his quarters. He was returned to Bucharest in spring 1946 and held in Jilava Prison.

In May 1946, Ion Antonescu was prosecuted in the first in a series of People's Tribunals, on charges of war crimes, crimes against the peace and treason, economic exploitation of the Jewish community, responsibility for the pogroms of Odessa and Iasi, the deportations of Jews to Transnistria and the direct involvement of the killing of thousands of Jews in Romania.

He was found guilty on all charges. Together with his co-defendants Mihai Antonescu, Alexianu and Vasiliu, the former conducător was executed by a military firing squad on June 1, 1946. Now that the war was behind us, we had to deal with the menacing situation back home. The balance of power in Israel had changed. The Jewish population expanded and, by the end of the war, its objectives were no longer compatible with the aims of British rule. Now we had to protect the Beit Hakerem neighborhood from harassment by the inhabitants of the Arab villages around us, which was constantly increasing.

As Beit Hakerem expended, David Yellin teachers' seminar marked the edge of the neighborhood, and we set up guard posts on the roof to drive away pillagers who came from the direction of Deir Yassin trying to disrupt our daily lives.

CHAPTER 26

Defending the Country

Defending the neighborhood was not enough. It was merely a locally organized group against an increasingly growing threat. The Jewish settlement had come to terms with the fact that the British government was not going to protect them. The British regime had returned to its original position before the war - supporting the White Paper restricting the immigration of Jews to Palestine and limiting Jewish settlement. We knew of the horrors that had taken place in Europe and from which we had managed to escape, and I was determined to do anything to facilitate the immigration of Jews from Europe without restrictions. That was why my father and I joined the Haganah, the Jewish paramilitary organization in British Mandate Palestine. My father served in the guard corps and I became a field soldier.

I took advantage of my military training to get more involved in the underground activities of the Haganah. At first it was only a few days a week, but as time went on the activities grew bigger. I participated in the break-in at the Atlit camp, the same camp where we were detained when we first came to Israel. We released the immigrants who were still being held there. This symbolized to me most of all, that we have made a difference.

On the evening of November 29, 1947, when the vote at the UN General Assembly ended the British Mandate and cleared the way for the establishment of a Jewish state and an Arab state in Palestine, fierce battles broke out in Jerusalem. The Arab troops launched attacks on civilian targets and tried to isolate Jewish settlements. The Haganah troops, my father and I among them, launched an organized counterattack, in which we captured the Arab village of Deir Yassin and put an end to attacks on Beit Hakerem. Katamon neighborhood and the village Lifta were also captured. We tried to break the siege of Jerusalem in Operation "Nachshon" and Operation "Yevusi", and we partly succeeded. We took over the entire area west of Latrun ridge, but then the inevitable happened. The British Mandate was officially ended on May 15, 1948. It was a Friday night, so to avoid breaking the Sabbath, the people's council decided to convene on Friday, May 14, and David Ben-Gurion's profound and moving words declaring statehood were heard on the radio on the Kol Israel station:

"Accordingly we, members of the people's council [...] hereby declare the establishment of a Jewish state in Eretz-Israel, to be known as the state of Israel."

The invasion of Five Arab armies had begun. Egypt, Jordan, Lebanon, Syria, and Iraq. As we were now part of the new Israel Defense Forces, we tried to stop the Jordanian Arab Legion in Jerusalem, in the same fashion we had taken Latrun ridge. Death was looming, but we fought for our destiny, for our homes and families.

The Siege of Jerusalem was hard. The first truce came about in June 1948. Then fighting resumed, then a second truce, and finally in December of that year, a cease-fire was agreed upon with the Arab Legion, and Jerusalem was divided. The municipal line divided Jerusalem: East Jerusalem, including the Old City and the Western Wall, was in the hands of the Jordanians, and west Jerusalem was in ours. Once again, we could return to a certain daily routine. Many lives were lost, and we hoped fighting days were behind us. The neighborhoods around us grew, and were filled with refugees and immigrants. Deir Yassin was in our hands, as was Ein Karem, and transit camps were set up to accommodate the tens of thousands of immigrants who arrived before the heavy snowfall of 1950. Massive building began to expand existing neighborhoods and develop new ones. Jerusalem overflowed with clerks, refugees, soldiers, and new immigrants from many different countries and areas. They came from all over Europe, Turkey and North Africa, but whenever we heard new immigrants speaking Romanian, we were always excited, and I had a foolish glimmer of hope that I would suddenly turn around and see the faces of Maria, Gabriel and the children…

My father had become the manager of the Anglo-Palestine Bank, my mother took care of the household, and Catia, Lili, and I began our academic studies.

Catia would sometimes travel to help with the absorption of new immigrants after the representatives of the British regime left; "so that they would come into our country with a smile…" she would say.

One day a man saw her working among the other volunteers, talking to the new immigrants.

He asked her what she was doing, and she explained that the girls were helping with the immigrants because there was no one to do it. "These poor people, who come into the country with such great hope, just get a piece of paper and are left to find their way on their own. I come here so they will have someone smiling at them, welcoming them, someone to explain how and what to do to integrate into society."

"Absolutely. Yes." After a moment, the man added, "I would like to interest you in something."

The man who spoke with Catia was a director at the Ministry of Absorption. He was looking for ways to make immigrant absorption into Israeli society more efficient. He saw how devoted Catia was, and took her under his wing. She began working professionally at the absorption center and helped take care of countless immigrants with endless dedication.

Lili, who had begun her studies before us, completed law school. Catia and I had our first daughter, Sarah. Three years later, Doron was born. Lili met a nice man from Tel Aviv named Ehud. They were married, and soon their son Ethan was born.

About two years after Lili, I finished my studies as an engineer and started working for a big company. Throughout these many years, we never stopped sending letters to Romania, but there were no responses and we began to lose hope. We didn't dare talk about it, but we were afraid something had happened.

Jerusalem continued growing, but in 1967 war broke out and once again there were fierce battles between the IDF and the Jordanian legions. There was heavy fighting to take the Jordanian positions in the city, including the famous battle at Ammunition Hill. By the end of that short war, called the Six-Day War, we had captured the Old City and Jerusalem was liberated.

25 years had passed since we had arrived in Israel. Twenty-five had gone by since we left Romania. We had always

reminisced about our times in Romania, but with time it became harder and harder to be reminded that we had lost them forever, and little by little, we stopped talking about it. But I still would dream about them every few days. Catia's house, Nelu's birthday, Rita's bright smile when she took the candy from me, the healing of the deathly ill Dinu, Lizica - how much she loved my father, Nicu and Doru, all they did to help us all survive, Matei...who made the biggest sacrifice of them all. They had become distant memories, almost as if it was all but a dream.

CHAPTER 27

Nelu

I stormed into the house, careful to avoid touching my father's body just as one would avoid touching a puddle of urine, and ran toward my shocked sister. She got up from the sofa, and a few seconds passed while we just stood there, silently looking at each other. I was waiting for her reaction, since I didn't know how they would welcome me. I thought maybe they had given up hope of ever hearing from me, or maybe they were angry with me over the years and did not want to see me. Maybe I will get a slap and have to go away in shame... but instead we fell into each other's arms. How good it was to remember Anna's embrace! How good to know she still loved me, and that most of all, it was not too late.

"Don't worry Anna; no one will hurt you anymore."

"Nelu, we waited so long, is it really you?!," she said in tears, "I never stopped believing!"

I let go of Anna for a moment and took a step back to check on my father. He still lay unconscious on the doorstep.

"Anna," I looked at her again, "let me see how beautiful you are. Will you ever forgive me for taking so long? Please believe me that in all these years, there wasn't a day I haven't thought about you!"

"At the beginning, I was so angry with you Nelu, but as time went by, the anger faded, and I just missed you all the time. I began to believe you were gone for good, and I lost hope that I will see you again, I lost hope Mama would get better, I lost hope.

"I will never leave again Anna, that I promise you".

We don't have much time, Anna, the old drunk will wake up, and I don't want us to be here."

"What... what do you mean?... What do you mean you don't want us to be here?"

"Let's start by telling me where Mama is."

"She's inside, in her room... but Nelu..."

I started to go to the room, but Anna grabbed my arm.

"Nelu, she's changed... she is not how she used to be... she has gotten weaker... since you left."

I opened the door of the room. My mother sat in her robe on the rocking chair in front of the window. She was knitting a sweater. Her hair was uncombed and wild. I went to her and took her hand gently.

"Mama, it's Nelu, I came for you. I came to take you away."

She stopped knitting for a moment, looked up at my face, how long I had waited for our eyes once again to meet, but she just looked down and went back to her knitting.

"Mama, it's Nelu; don't you recognize your son?"

Anna came into the room.

"Nelu, she doesn't recognize you. She's been like this for a long time, we just let her knit, and it's what she does most of the time."

I bent down to look closely into my mother's eyes.

"Elena, Elena!" I called out to her. She looked up from her sweater and looked at me again.

"Elena, it's me, Nelu, your son."

I kept trying. I felt that something of her was still there; something of her would remember me.

She looked up at me and her eyes suddenly widened.

"Nelu, it's good you came, I'll finish my knitting and make you something to eat, all right, darling?" and she went back to knitting the sweater. I was shattered to see her like that, but we had to hurry.

I held my sister's shoulder gently.

"You're both coming with me."

"What? How?... Where are we going?"

"Take everything you can with you, and do not worry. You are coming with me."

"We can't just get up and leave, where will we go?"

"I told you I would come back for you, Anna. Trust me, you're coming with me."

"But what shall I take, Nelu, there is so much..."

"Anna, we have to take what we can and get out of here as soon as possible, because if this fool wakes up, it will be either me or him…"

Anna brought out three large bags, and together we began to stuff them with things from the house.

We took all we could while my mother continued to sit and knit. I asked Anna to gather my mother's things while I got her up from the rocking chair.

I went back to my mother.

"Come on, Mama, you're going to move to a new house, much nicer. You'll have plenty of room to knit, you can continue there later."

She looked at me again.

"What is it, Nelu, are you hungry? I will make you something to eat."

I stood there helpless, but than an idea came to me.

"Yes, Mama, I'm hungry, could you please make something to eat?"

She stopped knitting and looked up at me, "Let's see what we have."

When she got up, I put my hand on her shoulder.

"You know what, Mama? Today I'll take you out to eat, what do you say?"

"Take me out to eat? Where will you get the money, little Nelu?"

"I have money, Mama, will you let me invite you?"

"But you must keep your money, Nelu."

"It's all right, Mama, I can allow myself to take my mom out to eat."

"I have to put something on then!"

"No Mama, it's okay, we will take your clothes with us and you can change before we go to eat."

"Why are you taking bags?" she asked Anna and me.

"Because we're moving to a new home."

That was a mistake…

"…new home - I can't leave the house without my things!"

She began looking in the bedroom closet even though I told her we had packed everything.

"My things!" she repeated.

"Everything is already packed, Mama, everything is in the bags."

She moved me out of her way and went into the room she had just left. She picked up the knitting needles on the rocking chair and the sweaters and woolen hats that lay next to them and hugged them tightly.

"My things, I made them for Anna and you."

Then we understood. We put it all in with the rest of the things in our bags. I asked Anna to watch mother while I dragged my father's still unconscious body to the couch. I did not care about him, it was for my mother - I didn't want her to see him on the floor on the way out and maybe feel something was wrong and regret leaving. Anna and I took the bags and led my mother out.

During the long minutes we waited at the train station, I was afraid the old drunk would appear, but he was nowhere in sight. The train arrived and we boarded. When the train pulled out of the station, I was finally able to take a long breath and relax.

We arrived in Bucharest and I brought them to the little apartment.

"From now on this is our house. I know it doesn't look like much now, but we're going to fix it up and make it nice. What do you say?"

Anna smiled.

"This will be the nicest apartment in Bucharest."

"What do you say, Mama?"

My mother looked at us and we waited for her words.

Finally, she uttered, "Didn't you say you were inviting me out to eat?"

Anna and I looked at each other and laughed. Suddenly all the pent up tension was released.

"Yes, Mama, let's go eat."

I took my mother and sister to Alex's Cofetarie. I introduced them to Alex and put them at one of the best tables in the cofetarie.

"Mama, order anything you want, anything."

"I only want coffee, Nelu, coffee with some cookies to eat…"

"I'll bring you all the cookies, Mama, all the cookies in the world," and then… just for a split second… she smiled.

The next day I went back to work at the cofetarie. Anna took care of decorating the apartment and watching over our mother. We took some of the old furniture Alex had in the back of the cofetarie and little by little, we fixed up the apartment. We slept on mattresses for the first few months, until Alex managed to get us some real beds. Every day I would get up early, pass by Alex's house and have coffee with him before we left for work together.

In the evenings, we would lock up together and go back to Alex's house. My mother and sister would come and wait for us with Laura and Luci, and together we would all sit down to dinner. It was the happiest time in my life.

One day, while walking down the street I stopped in front of a shop. Something had caught my eye in the shop window. With no hesitation, I went in and bought it. When I got home, after my mother and sister went to sleep, I took out what I bought from the bag. It was a new cap. I had got used to wearing a cap on my head, but it was time to put the worn out cap to rest in the closet. I had fulfilled my promise.

My sister began to help at the cofetarie. Now that we had more workers, we set more tables outside, and the place was still full.

One day Alex called me over for a talk.

"Nelu, you know you're like a son to me, don't you?"

"Alex, it's a great honor to hear such a thing from you, you are like a father to me."

"You know, sometimes the work makes me very tired, I'm not as I used to be, and it's harder for me to be on my feet all day."

"Then sit down from time to time, you can do that!" I laughed.

Alex did not laugh with me. He merely smiled his familiar mustache smile.

"I'm tired of work and I'm not young anymore. I think I'll start going home earlier."

"That's a shame, Alex, people are here until late, why close up early?"

"No, I do not intend to close early, I want you to stay and run the place in the evenings."

"I… I don't know what to say, Alex… it's… a great honor for me."

"You don't have to say anything, son… but I want you to promise me something."

"Anything, Alex."

"I know you and Laura are very close. Promise me you'll take care of her."

"I promise you… on my life, Alex."

"So we have a deal," he smiled and patted me on the back.

I have never forgotten that conversation. Alex started leaving work earlier, and I was glad I could help him and make it easier for him. I was glad too, about the responsibility that had come my way. A few months later, on a clear day, Alex went to bed as he did all other nights, but he did not get up in the morning. He died in his sleep just as I remember him in life - with a smile on his face.

It was a great loss for all of us, but I was not going to let the cofetarie remain closed. After a week, we re-opened, and all joined in putting the business back on its feet. Even my mother would sometimes come with my sister to help. It was my promise to Alex. This place was his legacy, and I did not mean to let it slip away.

From time to time, I would look at my mother while she was cleaning, and sometimes our eyes would meet. Nevertheless, I never saw her smile again as she did that time in the cofetarie.

One day, at closing time, Laura and I were together to finish up. I paused for a moment and put my hand on her shoulder.

I looked at her. She was beautiful and smiling as always, and despite the excitement and fear I had begun to feel, I gathered my nerve and said to her:

"I want your face to be the first thing I see when I open my eyes in the morning, and the last thing I see before I go to sleep, for the rest of my life. I do not have much, you know that. But I have a big heart, and you fill the greatest part of it."

It had taken me two full weeks before I brought myself to say those words. Not because I didn't want to say them, I just didn't know how. Each time I thought of saying it, it had seemed an inappropriate moment. Finally, I decided to stop waiting for the right moment and spoke. To my delight, she agreed to be my wife.

Two years after the end of the war, Laura and I were married in the cofetarie. Alex was missing, but we all felt he was there in spirit.

It was then that I realized that something else was missing. Daniel, Lili, Clara, Constantin, Mitu, Rita, Lizica, Dinu, Doru, Nicu, Gabriel, Maria and Zsuzsika. My family. I had to see them. I went and sat down for a moment, trying to calm the sudden sadness that had overtaken me as the guests talked, laughed, danced and ate. Suddenly I felt a warm caress. I was sure it was Laura, and I had already planned a series of denials if she asked why I was sad… but it was mother.

"Nelu, dear, don't be sad."

For that moment, my mother went back to being the mother I knew as a child. Her mind was clear; I could see it in her eyes. I hugged her tight and cried. I could not believe how such a small thing could release such a rush of emotion. Even at Alex's funeral, I hadn't been able to cry. Suddenly, the toughness I had embraced from a young age was gone, and everything poured out.

A few days after the wedding, I left Laura to run the cofetarie and set out early in the morning. I had another promise to keep. It was time to return to Catia's house.

I did not know what to expect when I knocked on the door and Dinu opened it.

He stared at me for a few seconds.

"Nelu?!"

"Dinu!"

We embraced for a long time in the doorway.

Dinu ran out to the field and called Gabriel, Nicu, Mitu, Rita, and Doru. He shouted at them that I had come back. I went out of the house and saw them coming in from the corn-field. Maria, Zsuzsika, and Lizica came from the other house.

We sat down in the house and talked for a long time. We spoke of what we had been through, but I kept waiting for the Lupescu family and Catia to turn out. I was devastated when Nicu told me they had left Romania for good. I knew that moment I would never see the Lupescu family and Catia again. I will not be able to keep my promise to Daniel.

Since that day, I would visit Catia's house at least once a month, each time hoping to hear some news of the Lupescu family. But I was always disappointed.

CHAPTER 28

Aurica and Ionel Enter My Life

On August 16, 1952, the second love of my life was born. We named her Aurica.

My Aurica was the most beautiful thing I had ever seen. She had her mother's eyes so I fell in love with her the first moment I saw her. She gave a new definition to the meaning of love for me. The first time she looked at me, the first time she fell asleep in my arms, the first time she smiled, the first time she stood, the first time she walked... so many first times. Magical moments that melt your heart. As she grew, I realized how important it is for child to receive all this love, never to feel loneliness inside, as I did. I decided to devote my time to Laura and Aurica, to increase the staff in the cofetarie so I could have more time with them. I had Victor, my most senior employee, run the cofetarie when I was with Laura and Aurica.

Usually, I would be the one to close the cofetarie at night, but sometimes I left it to Victor, just so I could see one more smile from Aurica before she went to sleep. One day, when I was closing up, and already thinking of going into Aurica's room just to catch a glimpse of her sleeping face, a strange sound from outside caught my attention. It came from the alley. It was already dark and I had to strain my eyes to see.

I couldn't make out anything, yet I knew something was there. I went outside in the alley and moved closer. I could see a stack of cartons along the wall on the right. I approached, and suddenly the cartons moved. Someone small enough for a simple pile of cartons to hide, was there. I approached and stopped a step away.

"Hello," I said.

No reply.

I knew that underneath those cartons was probably a frightened child. I knew it, for I had been that child fifteen years before.

I thought of what I could say so he would not be afraid to talk to me.

"I won't hurt you, don't be scared. I just saw you were out here, and I'm alone and need someone to help me close the cofetarie."

I did not know if I was succeeding in calming him down, so I thought what would have helped me to open up, if I had been in his place - and I had been in his place...

"If you come help me, it'll take only a few seconds. I can repay you for your trouble with a plate of cookies and a cup of tea, what do you say?"

The stack of cartons moved for a moment, and a small gap appeared between the top of the pile. The gap increased, and a head with light brown hair was sticking out of them.

I felt a stab in my heart. I saw myself in him.

"Cookies?"

"Yes, for a few seconds' help. I just cannot do it alone. Come on, I will show you. What's your name?"

"Ionel."

"How do you do, Ionel, my name is Arnold, but everyone

just calls me Nelu. I reached out my hand and he shook it.

We went to the door of the storeroom, which faced the alley. The boy could not see it, but as I walked, a broad smile lit up my face. It took a lifetime, but I finally realized that Alex had tricked me that day in the alley. There was never anything wrong with the door, and I was about to do the same to this little boy. I looked up for a second, and I could have sworn I saw Alex looking back at me from the sky, smiling that mustache smile of his.

A smile, a few cookies and a cup of tea. That is what it takes to change a child's life.

I put the key in the door.

"You see, I need someone to push hard on the door while I lock it, otherwise it won't lock." I pretended to be trying to twist the key, but in fact, I didn't turn it at all.

"You see, the door isn't locked, and I need to come in and take things out of the storeroom and lock it up again. Help me. Press the door hard, as hard as possible."

He put his hands on the door, and then pressed his shoulder to it as hard as he could.

I waited a few seconds, and turned the key in the lock.

"That's it, Ionel, you can let go, it's locked," I patted his thin little shoulder.

"So what do you say about those cookies?"

He nodded enthusiastically.

"Come with me."

I opened the cofetarie and led him to the counter. Then I opened the cupboard where the cookies were and boiled some water for tea.

"Listen, I need someone to stay here at night and guard the cofetarie. There is a lot of room in the storeroom, and we can arrange a corner there for you."

I went back to the counter and handed him the cookies. He swallowed them almost without chewing. He was starving.

"Eat, boy, don't be shy, and enjoy the cookies. What about it?"

"The cookies are very tasty, sir."

"Yes, I know my cookies are good," I laughed. "I meant what about the work, would you be willing to stay here at night and keep watch on the cofetarie?"

"I'll be happy to, sir."

"Call me Nelu."

"Nelu what?"

"Nelu Nazarin."

"Then I'll call you Mr. Nazarin."

"That's fine. Call me whatever you like."

I used what I had in the storeroom to arrange a sleeping area for him. I could find only a few cartons, a cloth that had been used to cover pastries and was now in one of the drawers, and an old forgotten sweater in one corner of the storeroom.

"If you get cold put on this sweater, and tomorrow I will take care of getting a mattress and blanket so that you will be more comfortable."

"Tomorrow?"

"Yes, unless you're not going to be here."

"Oh, of course, yes sir... ah... Mr. Nazarin."

When I arrived at the cofetarie the next morning, he was already awake. I brought with me a mattress from home we used for guests, a warm blanket and a pillow.

"How did you sleep, Ionel?"

"Fine, Mr. Nazarin."

"Look what I brought you, it will be here for you tonight. Tell me something, Ionel, do you have anything to do right now?"

Ionel looked down, silent.

CHAPTER 29

Ionel

I tried not to move, I even held my breath, but the person who had come near kept talking.

"I won't hurt you, don't be scared. I just saw you were out here, and I'm alone and need someone to help me close the cofetarie."

Nothing could make me leave my hiding place in the pile of cartons, as much as he tried to reassure me. It was nighttime and I was alone. This was what I feared from most. A little alley... at night... I was afraid because I knew I would be completely helpless.

"If you come help me, it'll take only a few seconds. I can repay you for your trouble with a plate of cookies and a cup of tea, what do you say?"

As soon as he said the word "cookies" my stomach churned inside me. I was desperate. For days, I hadn't eaten properly, and hunger gnawed at me. I carefully moved the cartons aside. I didn't know if I would regret it, but it was a gamble I was willing to take.

I saw a man in front of me, his white buttoned shirt standing out in the dark alley. He reminded me of my father for a moment, but then I saw the smile on his face. My father never smiled at me that way. Suddenly, I was a little less afraid.

"Cookies?" I asked him.

"Yes, for a few seconds' help. I just cannot do it alone. Come on, I will show you. What's your name?"

He asked my name and introduced himself. I got up, shook his hand, and followed him in the direction of the cofetarie. I felt I could trust him.

He went to a back door that faced the alley, reached into his pocket and pulled out a bunch of keys. He looked for a key, and when he found it, he put it in the keyhole of the door and tried to turn it.

"I need someone to hold the door tight as he can so I can turn the key, otherwise it won't lock.

I went to the door and leaned on it with all my strength.

He still seemed to be struggling with the key. A few seconds passed, and I began to think he had better get it to work soon, because my strength was running out. I began to feel that I was losing my grip, but just then came the sound of the door locking.

He said I could leave the door and led me into cofetarie.

The man went behind the counter and came back a few minutes later with a plate of four chocolate-covered *fursecuri*[23] and put the plate down in front of me. I forgot all rules of etiquette and fell on the cookies. Only by the time I had eaten the third cookie did I see him watching me, I lowered my head, ashamed. I realized I must have looked like a savage. However, for some reason, he just smiled and did not scold me for the way I ate...

He suggested I stay there at night to guard the storeroom. I

23   *Fursecuri* = gourmet cookies

gladly accepted the offer, not wanting to spend another night in the freezing cold in the alley under the cartons.

In the morning, the man arrived to open the cofetarie and brought with him a large mattress, a wool blanket, and a pillow.

I got used to waking up early because of the noise coming from the street, so I was already awake when he arrived. I was ready to thank him and leave quickly if he wanted me to, but to my surprise, he asked if I would like to stay and help him in the cofetarie for a hot meal at noon and some cookies in the evening. I was embarrassed, but I could not refuse. I nodded and he smiled and invited me back inside for some *pâine neagră cu gem*[24].

That day I watched Mr. Nazarin in the *cofetarie* to learn what to do. He gave me *pâine neagră cu gem* and *mâncare de cartofi* to eat, and I helped him in whatever he wanted, whether it was getting things out of the storeroom or cleaning and wiping down the tables. Two other men worked in the cofetarie, but everyone who came in went to see Mr. Nazarin. Sometimes he seemed to work harder than the two workers put together.

The next night I slept on the mattress he had brought. After so many days sleeping with cartons, it was incredibly comfortable to lie on a mattress covered with a blanket... The next morning I woke up only when Mr. Nazarin entered the storeroom.

As the days passed, it became my routine, and I was glad about it. I helped Mr. Nazarin doing everything I could during the day. In his free moments, he would sit with me and teach me arithmetic, reading and writing. He would explain to me how to treat customers to keep them happy... and I felt a sense

---

24   *Pâine neagră cu gem* = Black bread with jem

of belonging. I decided to forget about the group of street kids I had hung around with. After the things that had happened the last few times I was with them, I knew I would be better off without them, especially now, when I had a place where I felt good and was wanted. It did not occur to me that those kids might not have forgotten about me....

CHAPTER 30

Nelu

I wanted to help Ionel, but I went slowly and carefully, as I remembered myself at his age: how hard it was to trust people, and how hard it was to reach out for help. One day I asked him if he read books, and he replied with a bowed head that he could not read well. I started bringing books to work with me, to sit and read with him. I explained to him what the books were about, and the book he was particularly interested in was Jules Verne's *Around the World in Eighty Days*, so we began to read it together. We started with just a letter or two, then next week a word, and a month later we were already reading a sentence a day. He would come to me and ask me about the words he did not understand. Ionel was curious and intelligent, and seemed to be just waiting for someone to take an interest in him.

At one point, I made sure that Victor showed him how to open the cofetarie. He showed him how to take an order of cakes and cookies and set them out in the cofetarie. He showed him how to set up the chairs, what to check on in the storeroom, and all the other things he could do to fill the hours during the day and keep him away from the streets.

I remember that day he was gone like it was yesterday. I

made my way to the cofetarie in the morning, as I always did; only this time, as I came closer, I was stunned. I could not believe my eyes. The shop windows were filthy and shattered. Fragments of glass, bits of biscuits, and crushed cakes were scattered all over the cofetarie. The cash register was torn from its place, lying on the floor, wide open. I ran to the storeroom to see if Ionel was there. The place was a shambles, and half the merchandise was scattered on the floor. There was no trace of Ionel. I didn't know what to think. Had something happened to him? Had he run away because he was afraid? After all, the child I knew could not have had anything to do with this. I forgot about the cofetarie for a few moments, and most of my concern was for Ionel. Maybe he had been nabbed, maybe he was walking the streets, afraid to show his face for fear that I would be angry with him for not guarding the place. I looked at the cash register; there were dents on both sides. It was clear that someone had banged it on the floor several times before it opened. I never left money in the cash register after closing, so the burglars got an unpleasant surprise. Maybe that's why they vandalized the place.

We put everything back in order that same day, but it took more than a week to replace the broken glass and equipment. In all this time, Ionel had not returned. The thought of him roaming the streets haunted me. I didn't want him to make the same mistake I did, running away. If only I knew he was all right, I would tell him to come back, that I would not be angry with him. Finally, I decided to go looking for him. After the cofetarie was back to work and the damage was repaired, I went out to the street every day for an hour during the workday and walk around, searching. These were the streets I had walked as a child. I knew where to look, but I could not find him anywhere. Some days I would sit on one of the benches in the square and wait quietly to see if he might show up, but it was as if the earth had swallowed him.

As time went by, the hope I would see Ionel again began to fade, and I preferred to concentrate on the cofetarie and the family. Yet Ionel was an open wound in my heart. One night I stayed alone and closed the cofetarie by myself. My thoughts were already with Aurica and Laura. Suddenly, I felt an overwhelming thump on the left side of my head. The blow knocked me down on the sidewalk. As I tried to recover from it, I was struck again. I lay on my back bleeding, on the verge of losing consciousness, my vision blurred by the blows to my head, and saw a large figure looming over me. I wanted to get up and stop him from beating me, but I could not move. My body would not obey.

The figure pinned down my arms with his knees. With my remaining strength, I saw his arm raised in the air for a final blow. Then I recognized him, and my blood ran cold.

"Did you miss me, you bastard? Thought I wouldn't find you? You took my life, and now I've come to take yours. Now tell me who the fool is."

"You," I said, "The fool will always be you, remember that!"

My eyes closed. I knew what was going to happen next, and it was beyond my control. I realized that this was my final hour.

With my eyes closed, I imagined a last hug from Laura and Aurica. She would grow up to be a beautiful woman, and I would not be there to see it. I pictured Anna and Elena smiling at me, I pictured seeing Daniel again. I saw us all together in Catia's house... and then, it was... over.

CHAPTER 31

Daniel – The Journey Back

One day, I stopped by the big cypress tree outside our building before I went inside the apartment. When Doron was three, I photographed him next to the tree when it was a sapling. Now it stood five meters high. I stood there thinking how quickly time has passed. I took our mail from the box, went into the apartment, threw it on the kitchen table and kissed Catia hello. Sarah and Doron were playing in the living room. I was on my way to the bedroom to change clothes when suddenly I spotted one of the letters we had sent to Romania. It had come back, like all the others, stamped: "Address unknown." I picked up the letter and looked at it. I knew at that moment what I had to do. So much time has passed and I hadn't kept my promise.

I looked at Catia: "We're going to Romania."

Catia thought for a moment I was joking, and smiled at me. "Are you serious?!"

"Yes, we have waited too long, Catia."

From that day, I began to plan the trip. I knew that for Catia, the return to Romania would be more difficult than for the rest of us, but it was time to close the circle for all of us. That evening, I went into the bedroom, sat down on the bed, picked up the phone on the dresser, and dialed Lili's number with a trembling hand. She answered.

"Lili"

"Daniel, how are you?"

"Fine, Lili, how is Ehud?... And Ethan? – Sweet and quiet as usual? – he's the calmest kid I know."

"Yes, everybody's fine. How is Jerusalem? If there is one thing I miss about Jerusalem, it's the coolness that comes after a hot day, the fresh air. Here, the heat goes right into the night."

"Yes... there is nothing like the air of Jerusalem."

"What's happened, Daniel? You sound preoccupied."

"The truth is, Lili, there's something I want to ask you."

"What's that?"

"What do you think about taking a trip to Romania, to Bucharest?"

There was silence on the line for a few seconds, and then she replied.

"I knew we would have this conversation one day, and I knew that when you asked, I would agree."

"That's such a relief to here you say that, sis."

"Don't go making plans yet, you have to convince Mom and Dad."

"Something tells me it wouldn't be hard"

I was right. It wasn't hard to convince them. I spoke with them right after I spoke with Lili and they sounded the same. It seems we all wanted to do it all these years, but we needed a trigger. We were making the journey, the journey back to Romania!

In a month, it was organized. Every day that passed from the moment we made the decision, our excitement grew, and finally came the fateful day.

Lili left Ethan with her husband Ehud and met us at the

airport. We took Sarah and Doron with us. We had never been in Ben-Gurion Airport, and the excitement was palpable.

The flight took three hours and none of us could close our eyes for a second. We allowed ourselves to speak freely about Bucharest again and inquire about its present situation. We landed at the airport in Otopeni late morning, about 16 kilometers north of Bucharest, and headed for our hotel in the city. Already on the drive there, we saw how much the city had changed. It was as beautiful as ever, but it did not look as it used to. Maybe it was the years that had changed her, maybe it was Ceaușescu[25]... We had difficulty identifying the streets we passed.

The hotel was in the center of Bucharest, so after checking in and a quick visit to our rooms, we went out for a walk in the streets for the first time in twenty-six years. How exciting it was. We were able to show Sarah and Doron the streets we knew so well and tell them stories about those times. I felt for some moments that I was back being that young boy who left Bucharest, but that young boy was long gone, and I didn't let myself get excited, not until I kept my promise.

Every place we managed to identify made us feel that time had stood still since we left -

Strada Piața Amzei, Strada George Enescu, Calea Victoriei... it was as if Bucharest had been waiting for us all this time until our return. We walked toward our old apartment on Calea Griviței . The building looked the same. We knocked on the apartment door and it opened. A woman in her forties stood on the threshold. She lived there with her husband and three children. We told her we had lived there about thirty years ago

---

25   *Niculae Ceaușescu*, leader of Communist Romania (1965- 1989)

and asked if we could go in and look at the apartment. To our delight, she agreed. The apartment had changed. The colors of the walls and the furniture were different, but the floor was the same floor we walked on as children. My parents began to cry. It was an emotional end to our first day in Bucharest. If it were not for the feeling that we were interfering with the family living there, we would probably have stayed a while to reminisce. We thanked the woman and went back to the center of Bucharest.

After stopping to eat in one of the restaurants: *Mititei*[26] with mustard, potatoes and pickles, and *Papanași*[27] for dessert, we returned to the hotel in the evening. My parents and Lili went to bed. The day had been tiring, but exhilarating.

That night, at ten o'clock, Catia and I went down to the hotel bar and ordered some wine. We looked into each other's eyes, and for a moment I remembered the day we kissed for the first time on the lawn in the park.

"You're as beautiful as the day you kissed me for the first time."

"And you're as much of a flatterer as you've always been," she laughed.

The intense emotions we had felt all day were poured into a night of love and passion.

---

26   *Mititei* = Romanian ground meat rolls, kebab

27   *Papanasi* = Romanian donuts

CHAPTER 32

Ionel

I will never forget what happened that night. Mr. Nazarin said goodnight and closed the cofetarie before nine in the evening. I lay down on the mattress in the storeroom, as I used to do every evening when suddenly I heard knocking on the door. I got up immediately to open the door. I thought Mr. Nazarin had forgotten something inside the cofetarie and had hurried back to the store, but I forgot our ironclad rule never to open the storeroom door at night.

To my astonishment, it was not Mr. Nazarin at the door, but Corneliu, Sandu, and Petru.

"Here he is... thought he could disappear on us just like that, but here we are!"

"Wha... what are you doing here?"

"This is how you treat us, Ionel? We, who made sure you had something to eat every day, who treated you like a brother! And then you disappear without a word!?"

"It's... I... just... It's not that I didn't want to, I just didn't have the chance to get to the square all this time."

He pushed me aside and came into the storeroom, Sandu and Petru after him.

"So this is where you spend your time?"

"You can't stay here; I'm not supposed to let anybody in."

"What are you going to do? Throw us out, your brothers? Come on, show us the place, it looks like a cofetarie from outside."

I looked at Corneliu and did not know what to say. I froze.

"You see, Ionel, while you were here in the cofetarie, we sat around and said to ourselves, where is our Ionel? We wandered the streets looking for you, worried about you, and suddenly one day Sandu sees you sitting in some fancy cofetarie with an older man, talking to him. We waited for the place to close but you never came out. We came back the day after and guess what? We saw you inside, waited for the place to close, and still you did not come out. We saw the man who closes up talking to someone inside through the back door, and we thought, that must be our Ionel. We thought we'd come and say hello after all the grownups have gone home."

"But... you can't stay."

"Don't worry, Ionel, we'll take a little look around and we'll go. I've never seen a cofetarie from the inside…"

I was shaking. I did not want to let them inside, I wanted them to go. Corneliu went inside and Sandu and Petru followed him. I went behind them.

Corneliu came in, walked behind the wooden counter and looked around.

"Show us where you sit with your older friend."

I showed Sandu and Petru the table, and when I looked back, I saw Corneliu at the cash register.

"What are you doing Corneliu?!"

"You just leave Corneliu now, let him look at what he wants. Show us what else is interesting here."

"Don't touch anything!" I shouted. I went toward Corneliu,

but Sandu and Petru grabbed me by the shoulders and held me back.

"Stop it, now! Mr. Nazarin will kill you if he knows what you've done here."

Corneliu began to laugh.

"Mr. Nazarin will kill us, will he? And who let us in? That's what I would say if Mr. Nazarin asked me what we were doing here. You know what? I have an idea what we can do for Mr. Nazarin. Can you open the register?"

"What?!"

"I said, can you open the register!"

"I never go near the register!"

"Well, then you leave me no choice."

He began kicking hard at the till.

"Stop! I really don't know!" I tried to free myself from Sandu and Petru's grip, but they were bigger and stronger than I was.

Corneliu kicked the cash box several times until it came loose from the counter and then he lifted it into the air and slammed it down on the floor.

"No! Stop!" I cried out, weeping.

"Oh, look what happened to Ionel, cute little boy, are you crying? Don't worry, we're just going to leave a little present for your friend Mr. Nazarin, and then we'll go so you won't have to cry."

He picked up the till and slammed it hard on the floor again.

"Stop it!" I screamed desperate.

He just looked at me and smiled. Sandu and Petru held me, while Corneliu picked up the till and slammed it down on the floor for the third time.

Corneliu bent down and looked at it. I was sure he was going to pick it up again, but he went behind the counter without the cash register.

He was no longer smiling.

"What is this?" He glared at me.

"What?"

"It's empty, the cash register is empty! Are you making fools of us?"

"I told you I never got close to the register!" I cried.

Corneliu snarled, furious.

"You lie! You know what I do to people who lie to me?!"

He leaped from behind the counter, grabbed one of the chairs in front of us, and flung it in our direction. I ducked and the chair hit the glass display case and broke it. I couldn't believe what was happening.

"Let's do a little renovation here for Mr. Nazarin, who left us an empty cash register!"

He began to toss all the chairs around wildly. He went back behind the counter and began to open all the drawers and throw out their contents.

"Stop! Please!"

Corneliu swung a chair against another glass case and broke that one too.

"That's enough! Please!" I cried out.

Corneliu went about his wild melee, ignoring me. He tossed everything that came to hand, then went into the storeroom and started throwing supplies in all directions. Fifteen minutes of madness, and the cofetarie was devastated.

Finally exhausted from his efforts, Corneliu signaled to Sandu and Petru.

"Come on, let's get out of here before someone calls the police."

Sandu and Petru let go of me and I fell to the ground crying.

They stuffed cookies into their pockets and mouths and ran outside and down the street.

I got up from the floor, looked around at the wrecked *cofetarie*, and began to run.

At first, I ran toward Mr. Nazarin's house, and all the way I imagined his face when he heard what happened. It had happened because of me. How will I be able to even face him?! I couldn't, not after what happened, I just couldn't.

I stopped and changed direction. I ran as far and as fast as I could, until my legs could no longer carry me. Exhausted, I collapsed in one of the alleys, curled up like an unborn baby in the womb, and fell asleep.

I got up the next morning and continued walking, to get as far away as possible, to escape everything. I spent the next few days on the streets, wandering, asking for money from people I encountered. Every man who passed by me reminded me of Mr. Nazarin. I was afraid I would bump into him by accident.

I did not dare approach the square. I did not want to see Corneliu and the others.

The days passed, and my guilt grew stronger. How could I have left the cofetarie like that? Why didn't I go to Mr. Nazarin? Why didn't I tell him what had happened? How could I have been such a coward? I should have faced Mr. Nazarin. He would have believed me!

I started walking all the way back to the cofetarie, but when I finally got close, I stopped one block away. I could go no further, and I ran away again.

The next day I came back and again I ran away. I wanted to talk to Mr. Nazarin, but I couldn't, and I was afraid he would see me. The days went by. At night, I would sit at a distance and watch him close the cofetarie. Every time Mr. Nazarin came out, I wanted to shout, raise my hands, anything to make him notice me, but I couldn't. One night, when I was walking toward the cofetarie, a scary man dressed all in black came up to me and asked me how to get to the cofetarie.

He reeked of alcohol and his eyes were red. Gray stubble was on his face and he looked threatening. For a moment, I remembered my father. I muttered that I did not know and moved away, but I went back to see if he had gone in the direction of the cofetarie. I saw him lurking outside, hiding and watching. But that night Mr. Nazarin didn't close the cofetarie. His right hand man Victor did. After an hour or so of watching, he left. The next day he was already there when I got close. Watching. I hid quickly so he wouldn't notice me. The frightening man was dressed all in black again, and was swallowed up in the dark, like a demon.

Mr. Nazarin went outside the cofetarie to lock up, and the demon started walking toward him. Mr. Nazarin had his back to him, closing the metal screen over the door.

Suddenly the demon pulled out a club he had hidden under his coat and move close to him. A fire seared through my body and I began to run toward him when I saw him swing the club in the air and hit Mr. Nazarin in the back.

Mr. Nazarin collapsed on the ground.

I saw the demon lean in toward Mr. Nazarin and say something to him. He lay still, not moving even a little. They didn't notice me as I moved closer.

I was only a few yards away, and I suddenly froze. I was to scared to get closer, but I could not stand by and do nothing. I waited. I saw the demon swing the club in the air again over Mr. Nazarin.

I looked around, saw a big rock, and picked it up.

The demon struck him again. Mr. Nazarin lay stretched out on the ground, and the demon raised his arm a third time.

I had to do something. I pulled my arm back, gathered up my courage, and with all my strength, I threw the rock, a desperate shot, in the direction of the demon.

I followed the arc of the rock with my gaze. I thought it would fall and not hit anything, but I dared to hope. It flew in the air for what appeared to be so long... I followed its trajectory hoping... and then it hit the demon right in the head.

He lost his grip on the club and collapsed.

I ran to Mr. Nazarin and saw that he was bleeding. The demon was also lying there, bleeding next to him. I sat down next to Mr. Nazarin, raised his head, and leaned him onto my lap.

For a moment, he opened his eyes and looked at me.

"Ionel?"

"Yes, it's me, Mr. Nazarin!"

I did not move. We just stayed there. His head in my lap as I held it to stop the bleeding.

"Ionel has come for my final moment," he muttered, smiling with his eyes closed. "Never lose hope in people. You must never lose hope." That was the last thing he said before he closed his eyes. I sat there crying for help, and tears were streaming down my cheeks. Not because I tried to save him and couldnt, or because I felt brave for the first time in my life, but because I knew... I knew that Mr. Nazarin had forgiven me with his last breath.

CHAPTER 33

Daniel

It was Tuesday morning. I woke up slowly after Catia had gotten out of bed and kissed me.

After breakfast, we all got ready to go see Catia's house.

We took 2 taxis to the outskirts of Bucharest and asked them to drop us on the side of the road that lead to the grove. The green fields and the grove had remained the same. Twenty-six years later, the same dirt road still led to the house, but we couldn't know who will wait for us behind the door. So much time has past. All led to this moment. Doubts started creeping to my head. What if the house will be abandoned? What if people we don't know will open the door?....than again.... what if...

I went to the door with trembling hands and knocked. There was no answer.

I knocked on the door again, and again without anyone answering. We shouted, but no one was there to respond. We decided to go to Gabriel and Maria's house and try our luck there. My heart was pounding. This might turn out to be the nightmare I wished wouldn't occur.

This time my father knocked on the door, and again - no answer.

He knocked again.

"Just a minute, just a minute, I'm coming!" came a rusty grumbling voice from inside the house. "People today have no patience!"

The door opened. It was Gabriel.

He looked at us and his eyes widened in astonishment. Tears immediately fell from them.

Constantin went to him and they hugged each other for a long time. He hugged us all after that, without words, only hugs and tears. We went into his house with him, and he asked us to wait for a moment. He wanted to rush out to the fields to get everyone.

A few minutes later, Dinu came storming through the back door of the house.

"Where are they? I cannot believe it!" he shouted before coming to the living room and seeing us.

"Our Dinu!" Catia shouted. Dinu had become a big, sturdy man. The only similarity to that little boy he once was, was his red hair and freckles.

"I can't believe it, you're really here!" He rushed at us all and hugged us. Lizica came in a few seconds after him. "Unchiu?! Is that really you?!". She ran to Constantin first and almost knocked him down when she threw herself on him and hugged him. Then Mitu and Rita entered, and two boys with them, followed by Zsuzsika and her husband Florin. We all stood, hugging and crying, looking at each other, laughing at the wrinkles on our faces. Time might have changed us, but it didn't change the great love we felt for each other.

Mitu and Rita had gotten married. The boys with them were their sons. Sorin and Codrut. Maria had died three years before as a result of complications from pneumonia. Lizica had married and had a son and daughter, Andrei and Sofia, both of whom were at school that day. She told us that Sofia was redheaded, and Andrei looked more like his father. Her husband, Mircea, was working in Bucharest at the time. Dinu had married a girl named Alexandra and built a house down the road. Alexandra at home with their son, Adrian. Zsuzsika had three children, Roxana, Radu and Luca, who were also in school, and they lived in Gabriel's house. Rita, Mitu, and the two children lived in Catia's house, and Lizica had a house not far from Maria and Gabriel's house.

I was so glad we brought Sarah and Doron so they could meet them all. They told us that Nicu and Doru had moved to Bucharest and were working in a factory. They had married and remained in the city, and each of them had three children. Then we all sat down to eat and stayed until late afternoon. I don't remember the last time I was so excited. I was amazed to see them all, speak with them, I felt like I'm dreaming. I was so excited, that I forgot to ask the most important question.

"Gabriel, what about Nelu?! Where is he? What have become of him?!"

A strange look came across Gabriel's face.

"You mean, you don't know?"

"Know what?" they looked at each uncomfortably as Gabriel laid a hand on my shoulder. "Son, its something you must see for yourself. Meet us at seven in the evening tomorrow at the Athenaeum".

"At the Athenaeum? Why? What are you not telling me?"

" "Trsut me when I tell you, you must see it".

"What do you mean Gabriel?"

"You must see it with your own eyes".

I wanted Gabriel to explain me everything, but Catia wanted

to go see the graves of Emil and Adela. I knew the importance it had for her, so I accompanied her without hesitation. We all went together. Gabriel and Maria took it upon themselves to commemorate the memory of Emil and Adela, and had made beautifully carved headstones for both the graves, and encircled them with flowers. When Maria passed away, Gabriel buried her next to them. Catia set by their graves and caressed them. We stood there silent, Doron, Sarah and I, and hugged Catia. When we went back to the house we realized how late it was .I turned to Gabriel to ask him, and as if he knew what I wanted to ask him, he responded:

"Tomorrow, Daniel, all will be answered tomorrow".

Tired – we drove back to the hotel. So much had happened, so many emotions burst when we saw them, and the next day, I was about to see the Athenaeum again.

CHAPTER 34

The Return to The Fortress

We walked in the streets of center Bucharest and along the Dâmbovița River the next day, but we were anxious and couldn't stop thinking about the return to the Athenaeum after all these years. In the evening, we took a taxi to the Athenaeum so as not to burden Constantin and Clara with a long walk. All excited, at last we stood in front of the magnificent building.

I was already over forty years old, and yet, entering the doors of the Athenaeum still brought back the same sensation I had when I walked through its doors for the first time, at the age of seven.

The Athenaeum had not lost its luster, inside and out: the splendid reception hall had been renovated and was even brighter and more spectacular - the huge marble columns and the high ceiling, the superb arches, the glistening floor with its many hues, the gigantic chandeliers that illuminated the hall... were as glorious and remarkable as always.

We arrived earlier than expected, at ten minutes to seven. We stood in the hall and waited excitedly for the whole party to arrive. Suddenly, I felt someone touch my left shoulder. I turned to my left, and there was a young woman of about twenty in front of me, with long curly hair and blue eyes. Her face seemed familiar to me, but I could not possibly know her, she was too young.

"Daniel?" she asked.

"Yes, do we know each other?"

"No," she smiled, "not yet... I'm so happy to hear you have come. Sorry... I'm starting to babble and I have not introduced myself. I'm Aurica, Aurica Nazarin."

I looked at her again and immediately realized why she looked so familiar to me. Tears flooded my eyes.

"You... mean, you're Nelu's daughter?"

"Nice to meet you," she smiled, and held out her hand.

I went over to her and hugged her without thinking twice.

Everyone came over to meet her and embrace her.

"Come, we'll have time to catch up, the show is about to start and everyone is waiting for you."

"Waiting for us?" my father asked, surprised.

"Of course," said Aurica, "you are the guests of honor."

She took us toward the reception hall, through the crowd, and then we met the whole bunch. This time with Nicu and Doru. Nicu approached my father.

"Mr. Lupescu, I promised you I would keep them safe, and I kept my promise."

"You sure did," said my father as he laid a hand on Nicu's shoulder and looked at him proudly. "You sure did." We all embraced. Aurica motioned for us to come with her.

We followed her into the hall and continued toward the seats. She showed us to our places and we began to sit down, but the most moving encounter I had waited for did not take place.

"Aurica... but what about... what about Nelu?" I asked.

"What, didn't they tell you?!"

"No."

She looked surprised at the group, then asked us to sit down.

"In any case, the show is about to begin." Another boy arrived, and *Aurica* seated him next to us.

"This is Ionel, he joined our courageous gang about 15 years ago, and now he heads the orphanage counselors' team." Before we could say another word, Aurica sat down and the house lights went out.

I yearned to meet my friend and hug him, to apologize for all the years we had not seen each other and tell him how much we had missed him… to see him again at least once more time. We promised to meet again… the stage lights came on while I was drowning in sorrow.

Gradually I began to realize something I should have understood the moment Gabriel refused to tell me about Nelu. Such promises exist only in the movies. Nelu was… gone!

Two people came to center stage, but I was preoccupied with thoughts of Nelu and did not look up. Catia, who was next to me, lightly brushed my hand so that I would raise my head. There was a man and a woman on the stage speaking about the orphanage named in memory of Matei Marga. The man continued:

"As we do every week, we shall all enjoy a concert by the Marga Orphanage orchestra, but tonight I want to take a moment to thank special guests who have come from far away and have made this evening even more special." He smiled at us with gleaming eyes. I looked closely at him, looked through the wrinkles, the mustache, squinted and focused my eyes… could it be? Nelu!

"Let us begin!" he declared, and the audience applauded.

I felt Aurica put something in my hand.

"He asked me to give you this."

I looked down at my hand. It was Nelu's old cap. As I opened it, I saw a note inside it. I opened the note and read what it said: "We shall meet again… triumphant."

The End

32287719R00122

Made in the USA
Lexington, KY
01 March 2019